Ellen Mattson was born in 1962 on Sweden's west coast, and is the daughter of children's author Olle Mattson. Regarded as one of Sweden's most important young writers, she has published four previous works of fiction. She has recently completed a sixth novel, *Splendorville*.

SNOW

Ellen Mattson

Translated from the Swedish
by Sarah Death

JONATHAN CAPE
LONDON

First published with the title *Snö* by Albert Bonniers Förlag, Stockholm 2001

2 4 6 8 10 9 7 5 3 1

Copyright © Ellen Mattson and Albert Bonniers Förlag, 2001
English translation copyright © Sarah Death, 2005

Ellen Mattson has asserted her right under the Copyright, Designs
and Patents Act 1988 to be identified as the author of this work

First published in Great Britain in 2005 by
Jonathan Cape
Random House, 20 Vauxhall Bridge Road, London SW1V 2SA

Random House Australia (Pty) Limited
20 Alfred Street, Milsons Point, Sydney,
New South Wales 2061, Australia

Random House New Zealand Limited
18 Poland Road, Glenfield,
Auckland 10, New Zealand

Random House South Africa (Pty) Limited
Endulini, 5A Jubilee Road, Parktown 2193, South Africa

The Random House Group Limited Reg. No. 954009
www.randomhouse.co.uk

A CIP catalogue record for this book is available from the British Library

ISBN 0-224-07266-8

Papers used by Random House are natural,
recyclable products made from wood grown in sustainable forests;
the manufacturing processes conform to the environmental
regulations of the country of origin

Typeset in Adobe Garamond by Palimpsest Book Production Limited
Polmont, Stirlingshire
Printed and bound in Great Britain by
Mackays of Chatham plc

SNOW

CHAPTER 1

As the door swung closed behind him he was alone again. The tavern where they had huddled round the hearth and talked, as bottles and glasses stood glinting in the firelight, was no more; what remained was the darkness of the deep doorway and a wind that smelt of snow. Blinded by the ice-cold winter air, he had to steady himself against the wall; and as the last remnant of courage was driven out of him he looked at the stars. His father had taught him their names, but he had forgotten them all, except that of the white star in the north. 'Polaris,' he whispered, rubbing the back of his neck against the brick wall as a vast bank of cloud came rolling in from the sea, laden with snow. He did not see it, noted only that the stars were going out one by one and the wind was getting up, making the lantern above his head swing and creak on its hook. All the houses along the street lay in darkness, but in the flickering circle of lantern light he saw the snow that was beginning to fall, suddenly and swiftly and as if directed inwards, at him. The clock on the town hall struck nine. Once more he looked for the star with the beautiful name, but the sky was now a block of darkness, punctured only by driving snow. The stars had gone out, the King was dead. And the wound on his arm refused to heal.

His name was Jakob Törn. One night in early December he had woken to the sound of galloping hooves, run to the window and seen a courier speeding along the moon-white street. He had realised right away what message the man on horseback must be carrying with him. The next day, when he told his wife the news, she had reached without a word for the knife that was still lying on the table from dinner and stabbed him in the arm with it; and to stop himself beating her to death he had rushed out of the room, down the stairway that was so narrow he bloodied the walls and out into the courtyard, where he had lain for a few minutes in a snowdrift. He had bellowed so loud that the snow had come crashing down from the woodshed roof. When he got up he saw the blood on the ground and that made him run, out into the street. Two weeks had gone by; he had not seen her since. But the memory of her face as she took aim with the knife often kept him awake at night.

When he moved he felt it again, the wound that would not heal, opening up like a mouth. To forget it, he had to slam his hand hard against the wall. An unusually vicious wind whipped snow into his eyes; he knew he ought to move, but now the cold had turned the mild inebriation to a lead weight inside him. His legs were of iron, his feet of ice. He launched his heavy frame with effort from the snow-powdered wall, then stopped for a moment and looked at the impression he had left there, beneath the lantern. It was formless, without a soul. It was as if a huge animal had rested against the wall of the house for a moment.

He turned his back on it and set off, rocking in his big coat with his stiff leg fully extended at every step. Drunk or sober, this was his gait, rolling like a ship with raised arms seeming to paddle the air to counterbalance the limp.

And yet he had once been a boy riding a horse, with a flag flapping noisily in the wind, a flag on which a lion opened its jaws and stuck out its red tongue in a grimace intended to both frighten and mock the enemy. Oh for that flag, streaming out against the blue sky, oh for the salty wind from the sea and the rhythmic movement of the horse between the healthy legs of the boy!

He was a big man, solid and broad-shouldered, with heavy features, coarse skin, stubbly blond hair already going grey, eyes the same nondescript colour as the muddy bottom of a lake. When he was angry, his eyebrows stood out as broad bands of white across his ruddy forehead. He was made for exertion, for felling trees, lifting boulders with crowbars, sailing in fierce winds, marching all day without tiring: but the work to which he was now consigned required no strength. What it required was precision and patience, qualities he had never valued in others and never developed in himself; but no one had ever laughed at his great, clumsy hands fumbling with tasks that did not suit them.

He talked to himself as he walked and his deep voice echoed between the walls of the houses. Any nocturnal passer-by would have made out words like star, horse, king and death, without pondering much on how they all fitted together. Jakob Törn always talked to himself when he had been drinking, when he was alone, when the picture of the boy with the flag floated up to the surface like a blue bubble. It was a beautiful memory, he contemplated it for a long time, but the instant the horse fell, the picture went black and he remembered nothing more.

Having his leg crushed on that occasion had troubled him less than people realised, for a stiff leg weighed light against the misfortune of not existing at all. He thought he understood what not existing meant; he thought he had just had time to perceive it in the second of the horse's fall, before it all went dark. So he measured out alder buckthorn, rhubarb root and theriac without feeling ashamed of their lightness, handled the little weights on the apothecary's scales, poured burnt almonds into a cone so small it disappeared between his thumb and index finger. He accepted the change because that was what happened as time passed: the great wheel spun, it spun so fast that you had no more than rubbed your eyes before the change was accomplished.

Which did not mean the other could ever be taken from him. The moment was still there, the blue sky, the blue sea, the flapping flag, the King's silhouette out at the point, thin and somehow corroded by the glitter on the water. And then the bullet hitting the sand with a hiss and the horse shying and falling. Life was still there, too. He was only thirty-three years old.

Another gust of wind blew, filling his coat and propelling him between the snowdrifts, but he did not feel the cold. He was hardened from two weeks in the draughty warehouse where he slept, in the tavern where he ate and drank and in the blustery streets between them. The little grey town squatted there beneath the wind, which like the bad news was coming from the north. Star, horse, king and death; he pulled his collar up more tightly round his face and heard the clock on the tower of the town hall strike the half-hour.

He was already late, but now the walk in the fresh air had opened a chink, and through it he could see the hand, the hand with the knife taking aim at his chest, the knife that flashed and was brought down so slowly he had time to take a side step. He did not know which was more horrible, the hand with the knife or her face that was severe and almost absent, as if she had been thinking of something else as she struck. In the tavern beneath the town hall he drank Rhenish wine, and at once a veil of sunshine yellow descended over his memory. He laughed for quite a time at one of the stone pillars holding up the vaulted roof and then went out without shutting the door, laughing at the angry voices sending curses after him. Outside it had grown lighter; he wondered what the explanation could be, whether it was the covering of newly fallen snow or the fact that the buildings in this part of town were larger, richer, better lit. He stood for a long time on the bridge, looking down into the water that never froze and being glad of the living, moving boundary of black between his part of town and the one inhabited by the Mayor, whose house he could now see some hundred metres away, shimmering like a cathedral. He liked the wide streets and light buildings. But he was used to the dark clutter on the other side of the river.

In the Mayor's house there were candles burning with steady flames in all the windows facing the street. Jakob handed his coat to an elderly servant, then stood swaying and smiling and waiting to be fetched by his hostess, a woman he had loved his whole life, just as he loved her husband, the sandy-headed Mayor. The wine had made him disposed to love. Then he heard the hum of conversation from behind the double doors and felt suddenly unsure of himself. He looked round for a mirror but found only sconces and draperies, suddenly looming walls, closed doors. He was bent over a tiny silver tray, trying to straighten his collar, when he became aware of the scent of her wafting up around him as if her skirt were a big fan and heard her beautiful voice, turning ugly when she said: 'How dare you be so late, Jakob Törn, how dare you!'

5

When he saw her, he forgot the distorted picture in the silver tray. She was powdered, but so sparingly that her cheek shone through with its healthy colour and its three small pockmarks, three delicate little bites out of her fine skin. Her hair was arranged in a heavy ringlet under her left ear. She had a yellow dress.

'I love yellow,' he said, taking the podgy little hands she held out to him. 'How dare you wear yellow like that, Sofie, how dare you when the whole land is sunk in sorrow?'

'Shh,' she said. 'Don't shout like that. We only lit one of the chandeliers and we only had two dishes at table, ham and salmon. There's no harm in seeing our friends. Mattias says that's what people need when times are hard.'

'When times are hard we must let the balsam of friendship trickle into one another's wounded breasts.'

'That truly was not his manner of expressing it.'

'No, it was mine. Poetic, don't you think?'

He was still holding her hands in his, and began swinging them gently to and fro, not knowing quite what else to do with them. He had already begun to tire of her and of her blue eyes that contracted whenever there was something she did not understand.

'Why must you always be so strange?' she said. 'And why do you smell so awful? It's past ten o'clock, it's my birthday today; what have you done to your hand? Why is your hand bleeding?'

He moved her aside and wiped his bloody knuckles on the leg of his trousers. Salmon, he thought, and looked towards the door, there must be something left. He had not eaten since that morning. Sofie spat into her handkerchief and took a cautious dab at his face with it, but he dodged aside and prepared himself in his own way by running his hand over his short, damp hair. 'Go then,' she said angrily from behind him. 'But tomorrow we will talk.'

Yes we will, he thought, and opened the doors to the drawing room, tomorrow we will talk, but this evening I don't even need to think. He saw the raised threshold in time and cleared it with an airy step, then tripped over the shadow of a little table with a fruit bowl on it. Toppling forward, he slithered across the parquet floor and in between the legs of some old gentlemen sitting playing at cards. 'There's a bear in here,' cried a woman's voice. 'Sofie's let a bear in.' Various faces, eyes squinting through the pipe smoke, turned slowly in his direction; various heads came together until their talking mouths almost met. Oh, it's so warm in here, he thought, and tugged at his collar as he struggled up, his other hand on someone's shoulder. 'Now listen here,' cried a cracked voice, 'what the devil do you mean by looking at my cards?'

The air was thick in the large room, the tiled stoves were glowing, the candles smoking and dripping. Through the doors to the dining room he could see the table being reset after dinner. 'You must be thirsty,' said Mattias Bredberg from behind him, and Jakob nodded and felt an arm with hard muscles beneath the fleshy exterior being placed round his shoulders and guiding him away from the card table where the old men were making the playing cards crack like whips and pistols. The bottles stood lined up against the wall, a hand with a dazzling white lace cuff raised a glass to the light to check it was clear and Jakob accepted it, drank, and looked at his friend who was so happy and had so much money. He closed his eyes and drank some more and heard the stern voice say: 'Steady now.' The firm hand planted itself on his back and steered him to an empty sofa in the darkest corner of the room.

7

Once they were sitting down, the fatigue that had been pursuing him for so long caught up with him. He suddenly lacked the strength to hold his head upright, but his thoughts were racing and stamping in there, screaming and baring their teeth. 'Quiet,' he told them, and leant on his friend's shoulder which smelt pleasantly of tobacco and did not flinch from his touch. 'You look a terrible sight,' said Mattias Bredberg, lighting his pipe. 'And I don't like guests who are late for my wife's birthday party.'

'I was delayed,' said Jakob, trying the alternative solution of leaning forward, but it was like falling head first into a well.

'How much did you have to drink on your way here?'

'Not enough.'

'It's a ten-minute walk at most.'

'But it felt much further.'

'Now listen to me,' said Mattias, bending forward until their heads were level. His blue eyes that were so much like Sofie's narrowed as he observed his guests, who were slowly starting to make their way to the dining room in small groups; he sucked on his pipe, which had gone out, and appeared to be counting the guests, evaluating them and their assets, trying to decide where their sympathies lay. 'In just a moment I shall tell the maid to bring you some food,' he said in a low voice, putting his arm round Jakob. 'They're all heading for the punchbowl, as you see, but that's not for us.'

'No, certainly not,' said Jakob, rocking slightly.

'You shall have something to eat and then we can talk,' Mattias went on. He shifted a little closer to Jakob's ear and said slowly, emphasising every word: 'The situation isn't looking good, you know.'

8

'Isn't it?'

'No. Don't like what I see, don't like it at all. But we won't talk about it now,' he continued, getting to his feet, 'not on Sofie's birthday. I know you understand me. Tomorrow we can talk.'

'What about?' Jakob called after him. 'I assure you I haven't the slightest idea what you mean. What is it you don't like? And why does everyone want to talk to me tomorrow? Why just tomorrow? How can we know we'll still be alive then?' An old lady with a white moustache who was passing by with a dish of candied fruit gave him a look of irritation. 'Well, surely one must assume that, at least,' she growled, and went to sit under the ornamental wall clock.

He tore his hair and tried to remember who she was. When that did not work, he tried to remember anything at all of what had gone on in the past half-hour, but all he could recall was a promise of food. Someone had promised him food. 'Well, surely one must assume,' he called to the wall clock, 'that it will be a bit of the salmon.'

The old lady raised her glass in reply, and at once a girl in a blue apron came up with a plate of open sandwiches. As he was eating, the room began to fill again, with elegantly dressed people bearing warm, aromatic glasses and little dishes of sweetmeats. Suddenly he discovered that he knew almost everybody there, that they were old friends, that he could make out their voices which were talking of such mundane things as the weather, the war and the price of grain. 'Feeling better now?' asked the Mayor, bending over him in a cloud of expensive tobacco.

If Jakob had not known him so well, he could easily have allowed himself to be beguiled at that moment by the plumpness, the kindliness, the slightly lazy voice, the eyes totally transparent with goodness. But he knew all this concealed a vitality that was formidable, almost overwhelming. He had seen how quickly Mattias could change and how lithely the thickset body could move from a badly packed bale of cloth to a hired hand who a moment later would be nursing his cheek as he was slammed against a wall. The softness was deceptive, like velvet round a sharpened knife.

Perhaps that was why he suddenly felt the need to justify himself. 'Much better,' he said, getting up. 'I was hungry, yes, that was all, because now it's gone, that strange giddiness. Look, steady as a pine tree.'

'But you're no cleaner,' said Mattias, averting his nose. 'Well, we'll have to put that right tomorrow.'

'There seems to be a lot to be done tomorrow,' said Jakob, and took a few steps to test his legs. They did not give way; he skated back and forth a little with a sandwich in each hand and had just begun to consider another drink when Mattias pulled him close and whispered: 'Devil take it, here comes Leo Fahlgren. And he's got his damned son with him. I can't stand that speck of filth running round my office day after day, spying.'

Leo Fahlgren had a large face with a group of very small features assembled in the middle, as if his nose were a magnet. He walked with a stick, leaning on his son and bathed in sweat, and called from a distance: 'My dear partner, they say the whole town is full of people from court.'

'Do they?' replied Mattias calmly. 'Well, they're not here.'

'Oh yes,' said Fahlgren, 'great crowds of people in need of food and clothing; that will mean money all right, and for us.'

'They will hardly be coming here to fit themselves out,' said Mattias. 'In any case, I don't believe we have the goods

10

to tempt them. But clearly,' he furrowed his brow and drew on the carpet with the tip of his toe, 'clearly, they will have to eat, of course. And drink, and smoke . . .'

'It's perfectly natural for the court to take up residence here temporarily,' said the Dean from over by the stove, where he was standing warming his buttocks. 'They all need to promote their own interests. Since,' he lowered his voice, 'since our King unfortunately died unmarried.'

'That's surely less important than his having died child-less,' said Hans Fahlgren, heaving his father into an armchair.

'It amounts to the same thing,' said the Dean. 'Ought to, at any rate,' he added, getting a little flustered. 'At least, in the higher echelons of society.'

An ancient colonel with rosy cheeks joined the group and said: 'Do I hear you discussing the Norwegian campaign?'

'Not exactly,' said Mattias. 'But we can do so if you wish, sir.'

'I haven't the slightest notion what's going on,' said the old man, placing his hand on an imaginary rapier hilt. 'Old now, worn out. They don't tell me anything any more.' He turned to Jakob and asked mournfully: 'Have you brought any news from the front?'

'He knows as little as the rest of us,' said an amused voice from the crowd.

'Can it really be possible?' said the Colonel, running his brown, dry fingers, light as balsa wood, over the dried blood on Jakob's hand.

'It's true,' said Jakob. 'I know nothing of the war.'

'He's got his own little war here at home,' cried Hans Fahlgren. 'That's why he looks like that.'

'Now do you see?' whispered Mattias. 'He's driving me mad, that one.'

The gathering around them had grown in the meantime; Jakob noticed several of Mattias's business acquaintances, a lawyer, a bookbinder and a young man who was something at the custom house. He didn't like their way of speaking from such a close range that he could feel the warmth of their breath. He vaguely contemplated the dining room, whether he could try to get out through the dining room, but as the little girl in blue ran past with an empty tray he jabbed her in the arm and said sternly: 'Am I supposed to stand here and die of thirst?'

He saw that this scared her, and felt a momentary sense of shame, but forgot her at once when he caught a glimpse between a shoulder and an unshaven chin of Sofie, walking along by the windows on her own. The feather in her hair was bobbing so presumptuously, she was like a sturdy little horse with a red-gold mane, a well-groomed, little chestnut mare. He knew exactly how her skirt sounded as she moved, like when you whistle through a blade of grass. She stopped in front of the window and his eyes followed hers, out into the darkness which seemed grey in the snow. Or perhaps she was merely standing looking at her own reflection in the black glass.

'But it's true, isn't it, that you supported the King?' said an unfamiliar voice somewhere behind him and to one side. He did not trouble himself to answer, for now the frightened girl was back with a bottle and first he had to smile at her until she smiled back, then to pour himself a drink without spilling any or trembling. 'Wasn't that so?' persisted the stranger as he downed his first glass. 'Weren't you one of those who applauded the Norwegian project?'

'Of course he was,' said someone else. 'But I didn't notice you protesting either.'

'Perhaps I didn't,' said the stranger. 'But better at any rate to keep quiet than to go around saying you agreed with it. Like him.'

'I haven't been saying anything,' said Jakob, draining his second glass. He had swivelled round a little, but still could not see who they were. All the faces looked the same now. 'What would I have said?' he went on, clasping the bottle to his chest. 'I know nothing of war, after all, nothing of diplomacy, borders, surrenders, treaties. I've never had any idea what it's all been for, this war that's been going on as long as I can remember. Not to mention this latest scheme, up in the mountains, firing cannons . . .'

'But if the King whistles, you come,' said the first voice.

'He whistled, I came, that's true,' said Jakob. 'I didn't care a jot for the war because it had nothing to do with me, but with the King it was quite a different matter. Because a king isn't a person. A king is the one who gives orders, who points, who says: Go. And so you go. That's the understanding, that's what's been decreed. You go because the King tells you to. His sole function is to be obeyed; if you don't obey, the world falls apart. And perhaps you do, as well. Perhaps that was my function: to obey.'

'And now you have lost it?' said a woman's voice.

'I've lost,' said Jakob. 'But I haven't damn well talked, no one can come and accuse me of that! The only thing I know about war is to fight when I'm asked to and die if I have to.'

'The most important things, then,' said an old voice.

'The only thing he knows about war is how to be thrown from his horse and sent home,' whispered someone who had not anticipated the sudden silence in the room. Jakob saw the words passing like a swarm of gnats on the very edge of his field of vision. They were blinding white. Later, he thought.

'But then you have never so much as been thrown from your horse, little Hans,' said Sofie loudly enough for everyone to hear. Jakob turned his head and saw her gliding through the group of black-clad men, slippery in her yellow silk dress, with a slice of cake in her hand.

'Törn here speaks like a true soldier,' said the Colonel and cleared his throat. 'And if only one has the right disposition, skill will come with time. For that matter, there are few who look as handsome in the saddle as our King.'

'The King is dead, sir.'

'Yes, he's dead. The King is dead. But he had a fine seat.'

'And so abstemious, too,' said the Dean. 'Slept on the ground, ate with his men . . . Not a thought for the good things in this life.'

'There's nothing wrong with thinking of the good things in this life,' said a grim voice. 'If the King had spared a little more thought for the good things in this life, he might have had the sense to preserve them. *And* his men.'

'They say there are five thousand trapped in the mountains,' whispered someone.

'Nonsense,' roared the Colonel. 'It's quite obvious nobody can get trapped in a mountain.'

'The snow, sir. It's the snow that's trapped them.'

'Snow, indeed. There are so many rumours going round. What were they doing there, anyway?'

The old man looked at them, flushed with punch, put his hand to his hip to challenge them all and, confused by having heard only snippets of the conversation, screamed: 'What were they doing there anyway?' Then the life went out of him, the crimson light went out, his head fell forward

14

and he had to be led away, pale and comatose, to be wrapped in rugs and taken home. But the scream was still there, transposed into a deeper register by the sarcastic, still unfamiliar voice saying: 'You tell us, Jakob Törn, you who have always been on the King's side. What were we doing in Norway?'

Just then, at the far end of the room, Sofie turned and smiled at Jakob. He raised his hand in answer as the men muttered and jostled all around him. They were waiting, but he felt he had said enough, more than he intended, much more than any of them needed to know. He would still never be able to explain the most important thing, the picture, the silhouette, the man out on the point, the blue crescent moon he carried with him in his memory, which in spite of its hollowness attracted him with undiminished power. A blue stroke at the water's edge, it was no more than that, and yet you knew it was the King; it was the King standing there, you knew it because the bullet that hit the sand did not unnerve him in the slightest, though you yourself were so petrified that you dropped the flag and pulled up your horse so clumsily that it fell over and crushed your legs.

'By Satan!' he yelled; and to make them see how tired he was of trying to find words for something which can only be understood through silence, he threw out his arm above their heads. A glass flew slowly through the air, but he did not know for sure if he was the one who had thrown it. 'I can't explain it any better than this,' he yelled, and noted a little heap of broken glass collecting at the base of the stove. 'I don't know if it was right or wrong, good or bad, I've never learnt the art of weighing return against investment, I didn't foresee the result, I didn't choose which side to be on. Because I'm not like all of you. I've always leapt without calculating the distance.'

'You're leaping straight to hell,' said Leo Fahlgren.

'Leave me to it, then. Leave me to be blind and reckless and take myself to the Devil.'

'But why would anyone want to be blind?' said Mattias mournfully.

'And anyway, you're not the one trapped in the mountain,' said Hans Fahlgren. 'That's the real hell, make no mistake.'

'There are so many rumours going round,' said someone wearily.

'Which mountain do you mean?' said someone else. 'And how does anyone really know that they're shut in if nobody's been there?'

Jakob felt the bottle in his left hand, nothing in his right; he lifted the left to his mouth and drank. No one was paying any heed to him now, and when he backed out of the group of men it closed immediately behind him, as if they were all made of water.

He stood alone, the bottle stinging his lips; sounds ebbed and flowed around him, but there were long periods of silence. He had never really known what they were talking about. Like a crab he moved sideways across the floor and overturned a table, a real table this time, with a bowl that broke in two. The woman who had called him a bear stopped laughing and rose to her feet in front of him with a large piece in each hand. 'You really are not fit to have in the house,' she said sternly, looking down at the broken pieces. Jakob did not hear her, he was heading for a corner. There he stayed, standing with his cheek pressed to a wall.

He remained that way for a long time and nobody spoke to him. Here, between a wall and a knot of agitated merchants, he found his first proper rest for weeks. He had never been able to follow their discussions, nor had he ever earned as much money as them. He was a poor wretch, blind to the greater design of things. Lame, blind and poor, with a wound that would not heal, he turned to the wall, bent double and whimpered with laughter at his own worthlessness. He thought he heard Sofie saying: 'Why must you always make trouble?' but it could just as well have been the sound of the shattering glass reaching him at last, like a wave taking its own good time to reach the shore. He remained rooted to the spot. The bottle seemed bottomless. 'I understand you very well,' someone said behind him. 'If I had a wife like that, I'd be drinking, too.'

The voice was hoarse, grey and rough. The man himself was hardly intimidating, merely ugly with his squashed face under a greasy old wig. They eyed each other for quite some time before Jakob said: 'But you already do.'

'Do what?'

'Drink.'

The other laughed a little over his punch glass. 'Poor you, Jakob Törn,' he said then, 'not allowed to sleep at home.'

Over by the stove, an elderly man shouted out that the war had cost him quite enough already; at the next table someone said in a loud, indignant voice that it was quite true the King had had very bad table manners, but on the other hand he had taken an almost childish delight in giving presents. Jakob leant forward slightly and asked: 'What is it you want, Wessman?' And Wessman went through his usual little charade, standing on tiptoe to get closer to Jakob's ear, cupping his hand round his mouth and even pretending to look round before he whispered: 'I've seen her. And I've seen him, too. I've seen them together.' His little eyes yellowed with satisfaction and his mouth, which looked like a crack in a wall at the best of times, narrowed as he smiled.

'You mean Lars Björnson?' asked Jakob.

'The notary, yes, he lives with her now. They keep candles burning far into the night. Others have seen them, too. And we're all on your side.'

For the first time that evening, Jakob felt something verging on nausea. It was not the man's words but the sour-milk smell of him. He turned away and tried to think as he searched for something to fix his eyes on, something that wouldn't immediately start swimming and going double. The room must be kept from spinning. 'Don't be stupid,' he said thickly. 'You've no idea what you're talking about.'

'Oh, haven't I? Don't you think I've been looking through the window?'

'I'm sure you have. So I assume you know that the notary's been lodging with us since the summer.'

'Aha!' hissed Wessman, wagging his finger in front of Jakob's face. 'But is he renting a room, or a share in the whole place? Is he renting a cubbyhole in the attic or a share in your wife's bed?'

Jakob extended his hand cautiously towards a little pedestal table. His urge to laugh was so overwhelming that he didn't know what to do. He had imagined he would be able to reach the table and lean on it, but it was too far away. Off balance, he stumbled a few steps to the side and then collapsed against the wall, bright red with silent laughter at the thought of the orgies going on in his home between a man who cared nothing for women and a woman who as far as he knew cared not the slightest for men.

'It's not funny,' hissed Wessman, bending over him.

'Oh yes it is, it's damned funny,' shouted Jakob with tears in his eyes. 'And you, out there in the street, did you get frostbite? Oh, you'll be the death of me. How many hours did you stand there? And still didn't get to see so much as a thigh.'

'You're behaving like a pig,' said Wessman, straightening up. The others were gathering behind him, a diffuse wall of men who had never shown Jakob any ill will. Their faces were as immobile and mournful as statues of saints.

'A drunken pig,' went on Wessman, 'living like an animal, day after day we see you here, staggering round the streets. Well, I feel sorry for you, Jakob Törn, being married to a woman like that, being so disgraced that you can't even go to see your friends without drinking yourself senseless first. But there's a limit to our tolerance, remember that. Come to that, you weren't good for much even before all this, and if we hadn't liked your father so well we would have bank-rupted you long ago.'

It had gone quiet in the room. 'Watch out,' said someone as Jakob got up, and those standing nearest him backed away. He didn't notice; he wiped his eyes, ran his hand over his hair, dusted down his coat collar with a couple of brisk strokes. As he took a step forward, someone put out an arm to stop him, but all he did was to knock off Wessman's wig with a gentle swipe. It went sailing across the room and landed in the lap of a young woman, who pushed it to the floor with a little scream of disgust. Nobody laughed. Blushing deeply, the woman looked at the wig which had ended up under a table, and lifted it into her lap again.

'But you're bleeding,' somebody cried, and Jakob looked in surprise at the blood oozing out from under his cuff. In mid-blow he had remembered that Wessman had had a wife, that this wife had died, perhaps recently, perhaps long ago; he couldn't remember, but a sudden urge to inflict no harm had stayed his hand and turned what was intended as a box on the ears into something small, something humiliating. She had been as ugly as her husband. He ran his hand down his arm, his wet shirt was sticking to his skin; in front of him he could see Wessman's face, glazed, as if covered in ice. 'Forgive me,' said Jakob, holding out his hand to the bare head that looked like a stone. 'Don't touch him,' said Mattias. 'You've scared him, now.'

'Oh no I haven't,' said Jakob, trying to smile at the older man, who was shaking his head and half choking with rage. 'Look, he's not scared, he's not in the least scared. Do you hear that?' he shouted. 'Wessman isn't one for being scared, oh no!' Wessman, red and distended with hatred, hissed something at him and began to force his way through the crowd. 'Let him go,' said someone.

Everyone averted their eyes as the little man snatched up his wig and stumped out of the room. 'He'll never forgive you,' said Mattias, but behind him, motionless against the wall, Jakob had already left the party. It had happened very quickly, without a sound; he had merely turned his head slightly to one side and shut his eyes. Now nothing in the room concerned him any more.

As the other guests formed small groups and the party began to break up amid embarrassed mutterings, laughter and calls of farewell, he was watching a stream of pictures passing before his eyes: a window where the candle stood burning all night, a spiral staircase, a dead horse, a steep mountainside with half-obscured footprints in the snow, a very ugly woman leaning across the apothecary's counter to buy liniment for her husband. The wind was coming from

20

the north and carrying with it voices, snow and indescribable things; a tattered flag flapped in the wind; a dark face he had always tried to forget turned away from him, and he suddenly knew he would die of loss and regret if he could never see it again. Perhaps the ugly woman and the ugly man, seeing themselves reflected in each other, had found the ugliness natural, even beautiful? The smell of melting wax was as yellow as in hell, but in the window the candle stood burning.

The long day was finally drawing to a close. 'I think it's time for Elisa to come and fetch me now,' he whined, and sat down on a chair that slipped out from under him. It slipped because the whole room was capsizing, the whole house had keeled over and the guests were sliding down the floor to the door, where they were collected as if in a funnel and poured out. 'Shall we help you?' screeched a shrill bird's voice, but he fought off all assistance and began the descent along the silk-covered upholstery of the chair, very slowly, so he had time to remember the route he had taken from the dead horse to the staircase so winding that you lost your bearings and bloodied yourself banging into its walls. It sounded as though a flock of starlings was calling and singing in the room, but the dark face was mute.

As the door closed after the last guest, Jakob's head hit the floor. He was alone again. Someone took hold of his feet and began to drag him; the chair came too, the rug came too, someone prised loose his hands and gave him a punch that made the pain open out like flower petals blooming several hundredfold in his stomach. He laughed as they carried him away, he laughed all night so no one in the house got any sleep, but the only thing he could think about was that he had left her; he had run, she had

21

CHAPTER 2

Someone was in the room, putting things down. He could hear someone putting things down, picking them up, moving them about. It might be furniture being shifted around, it might also be something as small as a glass or a little wooden box being put down on a table. Perhaps it was nothing more than the drawers of a chest being pulled out and pushed back in again, but the sound, the soft, regular thudding, forced its way into his semi-sleep and swelled into visions of expansion, airiness, change, packed trunks and wide-open windows with flapping curtains. In his dream he knew that nothing would be the same when he awoke. Then the room went quiet. He slept.

He slept for a long time, until those wonderful winter sounds awoke him: quick, crunching steps in the street, children playing and calling to one another, their voices ringing like axe blows in the cold air. Without opening his eyes, he could see the little puffs of white smoke from their mouths. He already knew the room was filled with that white light which is so much more beautiful than summer daylight, the sharp white light from the snow.

He did not want to wake up, he wanted to sleep in the white light, with the clean sheet pulled up over his mouth, with the sounds from the street and the friendly presence by the window as protection. It was like the sun, a hot, yellow spot burning through his eyelids. He heard the tiny scrape of the needle puncturing the fabric on the embroidery frame and realised she must have fastened back the curtain to let in more light, and was sitting by the window with her sewing to keep him company while he slept. He was asleep, but he knew she was there.

Or possibly he was not asleep, but merely pretending to be asleep to prolong the moment and this physical well-being to which he was so unaccustomed. He hardly knew, and left it to her to decide. And Sofie, who must have heard the flickering whisper of his eyelashes against the pillow, put aside her embroidery and bent over him, asking: 'Are you awake?' He sighed without opening his eyes and she said: 'I'm sure you are.'

Then she was gone; he heard the door close and sat up. They had made up a bed for him on the leather couch in the Mayor's study. It was all as he had imagined, with the sun shining in through the big windows and a fire in the tiled stove, an empty wooden tub on the floor, clean linen in a pile on a chair. The serving girls brought bathwater: the hot in a copper kettle, the cold in a pail. He took off his shirt, squatted in the tub and rubbed himself with soap smelling of roses and tar. As soon as they had gone he opened wide the doors of the stove and emptied the pail of cold water over his head, then leant back against the edge of the tub and watched the fire leaping among the dry logs, feeling his body grow warm and soft with long red streaks where the blood had started coursing.

When he had dried and dressed himself, Sophie came back with a tray. He sat down in clean clothes, drank coffee and ate white bread spread thickly with yellow butter. He knew

24

he had been angry the night before and why he had been so, but he recalled nothing of the emotion; it could not live in this room with gilded dust dancing in the sunlight, butter and roses and crackling, resin-scented logs, and birds of paradise embroidered on the piece of fabric lying cast aside by the window. Soon enough, this time of respite would be over and he was grieving for it already, as if the bright, warm room would be lost for ever when he donned his own old clothes. He was only playing that the room was his.

Sofie had taken her coffee over to the window; she was sipping it and watching him furtively. 'Are you cross with me?' he asked at length, thinking of the smashed bowl.

'I'm not cross,' she said, 'but I am thinking. That enough is enough. That it's time for you to go home.'

'You really don't seem to understand this,' he said, putting down his cup. 'She tried to kill me. She stabbed me with the knife without turning a hair and she'd do it again if she got the chance.'

'Oh, go on with you,' said Sofie in irritation. 'If you really wanted to kill someone, you wouldn't go about it like that, with a scratch on the arm.'

'What did she want, then? It felt real enough.'

'I don't know what she wanted. It's your business, finding that out.' Furrowing her brow, she bent her head to the embroidery frame and her lips moved as she counted her stitches. Suddenly, she threw the embroidery to the floor. 'You must go,' she said, getting up, 'you must go home, you must hurry, she's waiting for you . . .'

'Oh, she's waiting all right, waiting with sharpened knives I expect,' said Jakob, giving a laugh and adopting a relaxed pose, his arm casually slung across the back of the couch to show he was light of heart, taking it lightly, and to make

25

her stop talking. Because she wasn't supposed to talk; she was supposed to sit quietly so you could be with her in her yellow room and be happy; he had always just wanted to be with her, keep quiet and watch as she did those things that comforted him, though he didn't know why, like sewing or reading a book.

But Sofie wanted to talk, her hands lashed out at him, finding only air, and she cried: 'Is it me you're laughing at?'

'Certainly not.'

'Is it her, then? Don't expect me to believe it's her you're afraid of; it's something else.' She came closer, bent over him, took his face in hands that felt surprisingly hard and gazed into it. 'Something else . . . but what?' Suddenly Jakob saw she had tears in her eyes. 'Poor Elisa,' she whispered. 'Women are so alone, shut up in their homes, there's nothing for them but waiting, waiting and waiting . . .'

'She isn't alone,' said Jakob. 'I'm the one who's alone.'

'Surely you haven't been listening to that old fool?'

'I don't listen to anybody. All I'm saying is that I'm the one who's alone.'

Just then the door opened and a little boy punched his way through the crack. Behind him there was a glimpse of a tearful girl in an apron, who cried: 'I just *can't* keep hold of him any longer,' then turned and ran upstairs while the little boy marched over to Sofie and started pummelling her with his fists. His face was bright red, his hair was curling with sweat; without a sound he grabbed her skirt and rubbed his face against the material.

Jakob poured another cup of coffee and spread butter on a piece of bread, all the while sensing the boy's furious eyes observing him from the folds of the dress. 'My poor pet,' said Sofie, and lifted the boy up on to her knee, where he immediately settled himself, like a Christ child in a church, his back straight and his hands folded in his lap. He regarded Jakob triumphantly and then fell asleep in an instant, his fat legs sticking out, his mouth open, his fair eyelashes matted with tears. Sofie carried him over to the couch and laid him beside Jakob as if she were entrusting him with something precious or giving him a present. 'He's screamed himself into a sweat,' she said, wrapping the boy in a corner of the quilt.

Then she went and sat down again, drawing one leg up under her on the window seat, and selecting a bright red sewing silk. 'By the way, he was here asking after you yesterday,' she said, holding up her needle to the light. 'The notary. Twice, actually. The first time you hadn't arrived and the second time Mattias went down and told him. That it wasn't appropriate. That he should be so good as to leave.'

'Why wasn't it appropriate?' said Jakob, moving over to avoid the clenched fists and kicking feet of the sleeping boy.

'Oh, you know,' she said carefully. 'Mattias had to dismiss him from his employment, remember?'

'I know *that*,' said Jakob. 'That was what left him so badly off he had to rent a room in my attic. But I never found out why.'

'He didn't do his job properly. Firstly, he was a distraction at meetings.'

'In what way?'

'He asked questions; but he wasn't supposed to ask questions, he was there to take notes. Secondly, he was always making ink blots in the record book. And thirdly, he made strange noises every time he passed the King's portrait in the town hall.'

'Strange noises?'

'Yes. Or pulled faces.'

'Well, that won't do, of course,' said Jakob. 'Especially those ink blots, they must have been an embarrassment.'

'But it was later,' Sofie went on, 'after his brothers enlisted, that he got really out of hand. Then he called the King a murderer and his wars illegal acts. Said there would come a time when even kings could be taken to court and sentenced for their crimes. But Mattias didn't make a fuss about it. He simply let him go.'

'He let him go and freeze and take a beating,' said Jakob; but Sofie did not hear him. 'You just have to have faith!' she said, and stood up so suddenly that her sewing basket slid off her knee, and red, blue and yellow skeins of wool went tumbling like a rainbow across the floor. She trod over them and dragged them along with her as she went across to the couch and bent over the boy. Nervously she felt his forehead, his feet, put her hand inside his shirt and pulled up the quilt he had thrown off. 'You *have* to have faith,' she said again, 'that when they equip an army of several thousand men, pay for weapons and uniforms, give them horses and food and cannons and drill them in marching and obeying orders and advancing on command, and then send them over the border to occupy a town, then you have to believe there's a meaning to it all and some justification for the whole enterprise.'

'That's the way I see it,' said Jakob.

'And yet –' she broke off and looked at him; he saw something in her steady, blue eyes, some little thing that flared up and vanished, like when you blow on the embers of a fire and there is a momentary glimmer beneath the layer of ash.

'Yes?' he said. 'And yet?'

'And yet you can never be quite, quite sure.'

He got up and went over to the window. After a moment, she followed him. They stood beside one another looking out at the river, the deep-frozen street and the windows in the house opposite, which were coated in gold leaf in the midday sun.

'Myself, I've always liked Lars Björnson,' Sofie said quietly.

'Who gave you the idea his brothers enlisted voluntarily?' asked Jakob.

'No one. It was because Mattias said the opposite: that they were stupid swine who let themselves be tricked. Who drank themselves senseless at someone else's expense and then had to sign up as payment for it all. But he doesn't know them, does he? Surely one has to try to think the best of people one doesn't know?'

'You're both wrong. The little one got himself drunk, it's true, and lost a lot of money at cards. And instead of going to Lars to ask for help to pay his debts, or to me, he signed up for three years. When the big one found out, he went to the recruiting officer and signed up, too. Because they'd always been together and because he was used to looking after his little brother. That was how it happened.'

'Please don't be angry with Mattias,' whispered Sofie. 'He's working so hard. He's only thinking of what's best for everyone.'

'There must be a lot of other things he thinks about, too,' said Jakob, staring straight ahead, out through the thick fronds of ice that were covering half the window. 'Sawmills and ships, and timber to be brought down from Värmland, and cloth to be shipped over from England. And finest lace for selling in the elegant shop on the square and ordinary lace for selling on the other side of town . . .'

'What of it?' she said, putting her hand on the window pane. 'He accumulates and builds and lays down stores and invests; he likes plans and blueprints, anything new. What of it? He works because he enjoys it, for the children's sake, because he likes money, fine clothes, food and wine and warmth; what of it? Would you claim to be any different? At least he doesn't let anyone down. He pursues a straight course.'

She had melted a hole in the ice flowers. 'A straight course,' said Jakob. 'That's what's so odd. It's exactly as if he knew where he was heading, and how can he know that? Most people just run from one sunny spot to the next. They chase the sunny spots. Run across great open fields just because it seems brighter on the far side, run and run until they forget where they were going. When they look back, their tracks zigzag and cut across themselves and disintegrate. All they've achieved is a trampled bit of ground.'

On the street corner opposite, a man in dark clothes stopped and turned his face to the sun. 'I just mean to say that it must be bloody annoying working for Mattias,' said Jakob, and drew smartly back from the window, 'because he's never tempted and never blinded.'

'Not everyone need be the same,' said Sofie.

She spun round and gathered up her skirts, stroking his arm as she passed him. He jumped and backed a little further from the window. Behind him he could hear her whistling and rummaging, a cupboard door opening, the long sound of a piece of cloth being torn in two; but when he looked round she was standing bent over the boy again, and the face she turned up to him had grown empty in an instant. Her eyes seemed virtually transparent as the light fell on them. 'Come here,' she said, winding a strip of cloth round and round her wrists, 'listen to him for me, is he breathing strangely? Surely he's breathing a little strangely?' He saw she was running her tongue round the edge of her mouth like a frightened cat. 'Come here!' she cried, and Jakob got down on his knees and carefully pressed his cold ear to the pale little marzipan-coloured chest, rising among the bedclothes. 'He's breathing exactly as he should,' he said, and got to his feet.

'He's well?' she said, and everything flooded back into her face.

'Yes, yes, he's well.'

She put her hand on the boy's forehead, ran her fingers through his hair, gave it a gentle tug without waking him up. Then she took the piece of cloth she had thrown aside on the table and went on tearing it into strips. 'Now it's your turn,' she said. 'You've been going around pulling faces for quite long enough. Take off your shirt.'

He did as he was told and bared the long cut on his upper arm, and she looked at it, sniffed suspiciously and prodded the swollen, fleshy edges with the cleaning cloth. 'You could very well have bandaged it yourself, you know,' she said. 'You're used to tying bandages. How do you think a wound like this can heal if it isn't bandaged?'

'I don't give a damn if it does or not,' said Jakob.

'Did you hear that, everybody?' called Sofie, as if the whole household were gathered there in the room with them. 'He doesn't give a damn about his wound!' She limped round his chair a few times and shouted: 'An arm more or less, a leg here or there,' but he let her carry on, for she was simply giving vent to her fear and chasing it away in her own fashion, by stamping on the floor and punching him in the back as her hair tumbled down from its fastenings.

31

She soon calmed herself, stopped shouting and mimicking him and set to work bandaging his arm. But she carried on scolding him: for not looking after himself, for frightening away her guests, for sitting in the tavern instead of going home, for being too lazy to work, for not listening to Mattias, for not listening to her, for not realising that Elisa was the best friend he could ever get . . .

'You're my friend,' said Jakob. 'But she never has been, never.'

'Well, have you been a friend to her?' asked Sofie, pulling the knot tight. 'And it was stupid, that thing you said about working for Mattias, when you let a poor slip of a boy mind the apothecary's shop all on his own.'

'That slip of a boy is eighteen if he's a day.'

'But he looks twelve. And anyway, that's not the point. *You* are the one who should be in the shop. If one isn't where one should be, then there's no sense in anything.'

'Perhaps that's what's wrong,' he muttered, and quickly pressed his head back against her body. He was ashamed of his sudden melancholy, hated it and revelled in it. 'I should have been somewhere else, somewhere else entirely . . .'

'Where, then?' whispered Sofie, bending over him, but he could not answer, he did not know. 'Just somewhere else,' he said.

At that moment, at the other end of the house, someone pulled a bell cord, and the sound migrated through the rooms to the yellow office where the fire had gone out in the tiled stove, the bathwater stood cold and grey in the tub no one had emptied, the boy slept, tucked up in a quilt that was far too thick, and Jakob sat half naked on a chair as Sofie stood beside him, waiting for him to say something more. But now the time of respite was over, now they could

32

suddenly hear that all the great house was full of sound, that someone was chopping and banging in the kitchen, someone was dumping an armful of wood on the floor upstairs, someone was playing a flute, someone was scolding a barking dog. Any moment now, the door might open.

'It's Lars Björnson,' said Jakob, getting to his feet. 'I saw him out in the street. But this time they seem to have let him in.'

He pulled the borrowed shirt over his head, straining it at the seams, and tested his arm, which felt whole again inside its bandage. The shirt hung loose over his belly and pulled tight across his back, but no one would notice once he had his coat on.

'You should have shaved, of course, I forgot that,' said Sofie, picking up the boy, who wrapped his arms about her neck without waking. In the doorway she stopped and asked cautiously: 'Will you be going home afterwards?'

'Do you need to know that?' said Jakob. 'Does everybody need to know where I'm going?'

She shook her head silently and he felt ashamed, but a few minutes later, as the man in black from the street came in, followed by a girl carrying a bowl of warm water and shaving things on a tray, he was sitting in the corner of the couch with his blue coat buttoned up to the throat, calmly drinking the last of the coffee. He had closed the damper, folded up the bedclothes and pushed the tub into a corner. The girl looked uncertainly at the two unfamiliar men and then hurried out with the empty cup Jakob gave her. Once they were alone, they scrutinised each other in silence.

'Well, sit down, at any rate,' said Jakob after a while, and brought his fist down on the padded seat beside him.

'It's much better that I stand,' said Lars Björnson.

33

He had halted in the middle of the room, between the wide desk with brass mountings where the Mayor saw to his business and the couch where Jakob was sitting in a ray of sunlight, legs crossed. He was as thin as the hand on a clock, as dark as his own shadow on the broad floorboards; he was almost handsome, but no one noticed that. People saw only the ruined remains of what had been: the hollowness under the cheekbone, the sharp edge that delineated the eye socket and made him look like a sleepwalker. Yet his voice was surprisingly strong, almost shockingly powerful for a body so transparent. His voice had been left him as a memento.

He was standing very still now, waiting patiently with his hands behind his back, like a schoolteacher concealing his cane; but Jakob, who had tired of the ceaseless interest pouring over him in the preceding twenty-four hours, got up, went over to the mirror in the corner, turned down his collar and began to shave. Through the soapy lather and the scrape of the knife he could hear the other man's breathing, which was fast and slightly laboured. 'What do you want?' he asked, squinting in the mirror. 'And why did you come round here yesterday evening?'

'I wanted to talk to you. I knew you were here.'

'You can talk to me in a thousand other places,' said Jakob, wiping the knife. 'You must see you can't come here when they've got guests. And anyway, I already know what you're going to say.'

'You can't know,' said the irritatingly calm voice behind him. 'And if you aren't in any of the places where you should be, then obviously I'm obliged to come here.'

'Even if the Mayor tells you to go to hell?'

'He's done that often enough before.'

34

'So what if *I* told you to go to hell?' Jakob asked after a pause.

'But you won't do that. You don't wish me in hell, and I don't want you there either.'

'I wish people would leave me alone.'

'They soon will. Wishes like that are the first to come true. Wishes should be saved until they're really needed, just like words. You're squandering your wishes on the wrong things.'

'And you're so economical with words that you drive me mad. What is it you really want? Do you want me to go home and ask Elisa's forgiveness because she tried to kill me?'

'No, I want you to go home and help Tobias make cough medicine. It's almost all gone, he says.'

'Elisa knows how to make cough medicine. Tell her that.'

'Tell her yourself.'

'You want me to be reasonable and placid again,' said Jakob, throwing himself down on the couch. 'Placid as an ox. You want me to come back like a runaway dog and whine at the door to be let in. But none of you know anything about me, you all dish out advice I haven't asked for. Mattias thinks I should get my business affairs in order; Sofie thinks it's enough just for me to behave nicely. And you want me to go home and pretend nothing's happened, everything's as it was before and I can hope for nothing better. You want me to give up hope.'

'No, I want you to go home and make cough medicine.'

'I can't be bothered to listen,' said Jakob. 'I'm tired of talking. What I really want is to be on my own, that's why I went off. Other people are a mystery to me; I don't understand them. And I've grown tired of trying.'

'One simply mustn't,' said Lars.

'Mustn't what?'

'Grow tired.'

'I've visualised it a thousand times,' said Jakob. 'Me going there, opening the door, climbing the stairs and going into the room. Her standing there waiting for me . . . and then I can't get any further. Because I don't know what to do next. Shall I take her in my arms or hit her? Shall I ask her to forgive me or expect her to forgive herself? She'll say nothing, as always; she'll stare at me, that way she has of saying nothing, waiting, not moving a muscle, not blinking, not smiling . . . She's like a stone, she's cold as ice. You know nothing about her, though you think you know so much more than me.'

Lars took out a handkerchief and blew his nose in a fashion that managed to sound disapproving. 'Yes, yes,' said Jakob, lowering his voice. 'But you needn't think I'm afraid; I'm not afraid of it happening again. I just can't stop thinking about the way she looked as she did it and that turns my stomach every time. It's not fear of getting hurt, it's the incomprehensible part of her, the inhuman part. It's as if Sofie were to bend over her little boy and he were to jump up and bite her in the neck.'

'Mmm . . .' said Lars slowly, returning his handkerchief to his pocket.

'Is that all you can say? Give me your advice instead, you're the clever one.'

'In that case I would say one has to assume that there's always a reason behind other people's actions.'

'Always?'

'One has to assume so, in any event.'

Jakob stood up and went slowly over to him until they were standing toe to toe and the other man's face was just below his. Lars's eyes were as blue as an autumn sky, but at close quarters it suddenly seemed to Jakob that he could look through them as easily as through a window, and inside it was much darker, much more cluttered and chaotic than you would have thought from hearing him speak. But you had to get right up to him to be able to see it, so close you could also see the fine pattern of burst blood vessels round the iris. 'You have so many ideas,' he said kindly, putting his large hand on Lars's shoulder, 'you talk and talk but it's all just air. It isn't real, but I expect you know that. You know you're dreaming and there's hardly any point in it all.'

'I have always believed ideas are real,' said Lars, 'just as real as what conflicts with them. Just as real as people. More real, sometimes.'

'And you're just as odd as her. Odder sometimes.'

'She's no odder than you.'

'At least I haven't injured anybody,' said Jakob, 'not ever.'

'Come on, there must be something better to say about you than that you keep out of fights?'

All the time they were talking, Jakob had felt as if he were sinking. It was because every word he said bounced off a smooth and perfectly crack-free surface; but there was another reason, more tangible. He suddenly realised it was Lars, shrinking under the weight of his hand.

'You look sick,' he said quickly, releasing his grip.

'So do you,' said Lars morosely, 'sick and hung-over.'

'Yes, but my sickness will pass.'

'So will mine,' said Lars. And as if to underline the fact, he fainted.

He took a deep, furious breath as if the air symbolised everything he had lost or never allowed himself – happiness, money, health, love, all the things he had never even admitted he needed – and then collapsed with a sigh that sounded almost content. His fall was like a bird diving, and Jakob caught him and felt the absurd lightness of his body and the quick, irregular heartbeats, which transmitted themselves to him, too. That tattered heart seemed to be beating its way into his own.

Then Lars spoke out loud and the moment was past. Jakob held him, shook him until he opened his eyes and carried him over to the couch. He held out the glass of water the girl had left behind; Lars smelt it suspiciously and took a tiny sip. 'It's stuffy in here,' he said then. 'They stoke the fire too much.'

'Where's the coat I gave you?' asked Jakob. 'Have you lost it? Did you give it away on some street corner, did you sell it? What did you buy with the money, eh? Ink?'

'That's none of your business,' said Lars, putting down the glass. 'I haven't time to sit here any longer; I only came to give you a message: Tobias says to tell you he has run out of cough medicine. People are very sick at this time of year,' he said pensively and got to his feet.

'I'll walk with you,' said Jakob.

'High time, too.'

'I said I'd walk with you, I didn't say I was planning to stay when I got there. Come on.'

He took Lars by the arm and led him through the series of interconnecting rooms. Sofie was waiting for them in the hall, though she did not come over but remained at the foot of the flight of stairs. She was watching a girl of about ten who held a puppy clamped under her arm while she patiently helped the little boy up each tall step.

'I'm walking Lars back,' said Jakob. 'If your husband wants me, I'll be at the warehouse.'

Sofie did not reply. She was absorbed in her children; with furrowed brow, she observed them as thoughtfully as if they had been two trees in bloom and she had been attempting to calculate their future, the risk of night frost and rowan moth grubs, yet without forgetting for an instant the present moment and the blossoming that was so explosively lovely and short. Her face was eager, rueful and inscrutable.

'We're going now,' Jakob said, and then she turned, took his hands and whispered: 'You must comfort him. You must tell him the boys are coming back. Now that the King is dead, the war will be over and everyone can come home.'

Jakob could have answered in many different ways. He could have said the war had outlived many kings; kings came and went but war stayed the same; there might possibly be a short interval, but it was hardly a guarantee of anybody's survival. He said nothing, though, remembering what she had told him: that there were times when she did not see her children, only the gaping void between them where the other three should have been, the dead children who were as vivid as the living ones and as much in need of her attention.

She had said it made her feel ashamed, that sometimes she was so ashamed she did not know whether she loved the dead children more than the living ones or whether she loved nobody at all. But there was a part of her that felt no shame, and this part would play with the dead children in their garden, which was big and dark and moss-scented. She said they were much as they used to be, only a little quieter.

She held his hands and laughed with tears in her eyes at the howling dog, squeezed tightly under the girl's arm, and the boy kicking the banister rails. 'Do you promise?' she said under her voice, over and over again, until at last he did what she was begging for: he promised everything would be

CHAPTER 3

The warehouse was down by the harbour. It was half full of timber ready to be shipped out as soon as the ice broke, fresh, newly sawn timber with an acidic smell of green leaves. In one corner of the big building, the Mayor had had an office built, and that was where Jakob was living now, surrounded by stacks of planks. It was like living in a forest.

He had accompanied Lars Björnson as far as the court-yard of the apothecary's shop before claiming he had pressing business and turning down towards the harbour. He had gone home to his own place, to the little box where he slept on a skin rug and fed the stove with bark and discarded wood chips. The only thing he missed was the smell of coffee in the mornings, but to make up for it he had the dull, sucking sound of the water moving under the ice and tugging at the piles of the jetty. On windy nights that was all it took to transform the warehouse into a great ship and himself into someone who owned very little and was always travelling on.

He did not know if he had ever dreamt of such freedom. One memory he had, just one, but he could not summon up any dreams. He assumed he had forgotten the dreams. He tried to find them again now; perhaps that was what he had meant by pressing business, for the only thing he did once he was safely inside with the door closed behind him was to sit on the bunk, leaning forward with his chin resting in his hand and staring out of the cracked window pane above the desk, out over the great, silent stacks of wood that gleamed in the half-light.

Having sat like that for a while, he got up and did a few circuits of the room. He put some wood in the stove, knocked a hole in the layer of ice on the pail and poured some water into a kettle, because those were actions that seemed natural. At home, you attend to the fire and put things on the hob. But he did not light the fire; he sat back down, pulled the quilt round his shoulders and went on staring at the little window as it grew ever blacker. Soon he would no longer be able to see the wood awaiting shipment to England, for which he felt a liking he could not explain. The wood was soft, it was alive, it could float, it could be turned into furniture, houses, boats or fire, but in all its manifestations it still bore a faint scent of the forest where it had grown.

As for him, he carried nothing with him. The days ran together when he thought back over them, thousands of muddied days with no distinguishing features, impossible to remember. The things he could see most clearly were those he had never done. He had never gone aboard one of the great ships, he had never seen an unbroken horizon, an unknown town, a foreign land. He had never read a book or set off with the open road stretching before him; but now he saw himself doing all those things, and the pictures of new people, streets, flowers, buildings and beaches were disturbingly distinct, replete with sound and movement and ablaze with colour. They were almost as vivid as the memory of the white horse, the blue King, the red lion on the flag, the soot-black bullet in a cloud of sand; almost as vivid as the only event that had really happened.

For nothing had happened since. Well, somebody had died. His father. He had inherited something: a house and a business. It had not cost him very much to learn to run it. He had thought he had no regrets, but now he was regretting the time that had passed, all those years that had grown invisible. The only thing he could see really clearly was what had never happened.

With the quilt round his shoulders, he went over to the desk and bent closer to the little window. It had been put there to allow the Mayor to supervise the loading and unloading, but he must occasionally have stayed on after the men had gone home, as evening came and the warehouse grew dark, and looked up from the accounts to see only his own face in the black glass. Jakob could imagine his calm gaze, a moment's repose before the face bent once more to the ledger, pen scratching down figures, forgotten pipe going out. He, Jakob, had no mirrors and seldom looked at himself, but Mattias Bredberg no doubt did so without agonising, in the same way as he did everything else: worked, haggled, berated lazy workers, ate dinner or played with his children.

It was the first time Jakob had ever tried to visualise another person's life. He did it to look for similarities but he saw only differences; for the difference between himself and Mattias Bredberg was as clear as the crack in the window pane. Fine as a hair, it ran across the glass and split his own face in two, like a reminder that what we see is only one half of what exists. The rest is somewhere else, cut off and inaccessible.

He pressed his knuckles down on the desk, rocked to and fro so the quilt slipped to the floor, took a walk round the thin walls, supporting himself on them and making the wood creak. He was too big for the room, too heavy, too blundering; he was too unused to being alone. He did another circuit and suddenly realised the strange sound was coming from himself, the low, rhythmic muttering that accelerated with his own footsteps and only stopped when he began clattering about with the door of the stove. But it soon began again; the other voice he could not control started all over again, laughing and complaining, and he did not know how to make it keep quiet other than by smashing up the whole room or crawling into the tunnels between the piles of timber to hide.

Trembling all over, he sat down on the bunk, then walked round the room, then sat down again, leant his chin in his hand and stared out into the darkness. All he could see was a grey streak indicating that the doors out to the quay were not properly closed. Out there were the last remains of the cold day, a sky still pale, stars perhaps. He could go out on to the quay and look at them and at the town huddled under the mountain, appearing from a distance like something tossed down, discarded, a jumbled heap of stone and wood emitting feeble gleams through mean little windows. He could just as well stay where he was.

It was cold in the little room, he could feel it now. It was not even a room, just a partitioned-off corner: two carelessly erected screens of boards round a desk, a stove and the rickety bunk where he slept on a skin rug that had been poorly tanned and smelt foul. He felt no longing to leave it. He asked himself if there was anything he wanted, but there was not, and though those foreign horizons he could see so vividly were dreams he had had and then forgotten, he no longer had any use for them. To test himself he skimmed one last time through the pictures he had recovered, but without feeling anything other than that he was cold and hungry. They were as lovely and as mute as the birds on Sofie's embroidery.

It was evening by the time he had made up his mind, but the snow provided him with light as he locked the door and made his way back along the row of warehouses. As he got closer to the town, their smell of wood, fish and tar mingled with the rank smells exuded by people and animals living close together. The houses too were leaning against one another beneath the mass of snow. Only the bell tower on the crag turned its face to the sea.

He followed the river for a while and then cut across the water meadows where the poorest people lived in huts of straw and driftwood. When he had climbed a little higher, he could see the town laid out more clearly around him, in straight streets and knots of buildings behind walls and fences. The smoke from the chimneys rose straight up in the cold air and descended as a fine rain of soot, and everything was very sparse: the columns of smoke were thin, the streets empty, the houses and courtyards silent and the windows dark. Behind carefully locked doors sat the townspeople, eating their suppers with an eye on the street outside and an ear cocked for the possible sound of horses' hooves and marching feet. They were waiting for Christmas, for spring, for good omens or bad news as they huddled together round small, anxious fires and ate thin porridge.

Jakob crept like a thief through the black alleyways. When he reached the apothecary's house and shop he stood concealed in a doorway for a while and looked at the house. It resembled a dark back that had turned away. Only when he was sure nothing was moving did he open the main gate and go into the inner courtyard, and it was lighter there, with wobbly yellow squares where the windows were reflected in the snow. He positioned himself behind two empty barrels and waited, and soon the door was opened by a short girl who came slithering down the steps carrying a bucket and ran shivering into one of the outbuildings. When she came out again, she cleaned the bucket with snow and then stood there, arms hanging, with her head thrown back. Her face was flat and white, like the palm of a hand turned up to the moon, her eyes two sharp slits, her mouth a hole. Jakob could not see the moon from where he was standing, only its light on the girl's face and the long shadow behind her. When she turned and went back into the house, the shadow flowed over the stable roof and vanished.

He was alone again. A few minutes passed, perhaps an hour. He stamped his feet and felt himself growing cold. Then the back door of the apothecary's shop opened, and instantly he crouched down behind the barrels and hid, for he knew that the boy had stopped on the top step, that he was listening, that he was looking all around him as if the moonlight and the empty courtyard frightened him. 'Is there anybody there?' he called as he did every evening, before turning the key twice in the lock and pulling at the door to check it was firmly fastened. He came gingerly down the icy stone stair and put the key in his waistcoat pocket as he talked to himself of matters he must not forget: something about a bottle and a parcel to be delivered. Jakob knew he was walking the few steps to the kitchen door with his hands behind his back and his eyes on the ground. Twice he stopped and felt to check that the key was still there.

They had found the girl in the pigsty, lying asleep with a crust of mouldy bread in her hand. The boy came a few days later, but he stood in the courtyard in the rain until Elisa ran to fetch him in. This was at the time of the plague, when there were children turning up in all sorts of places. These two had most likely come from some village where no one had any resistance to face yet another misfortune on top of a long-running war and three consecutive failed harvests; it could not have taken long for those people to die. Perhaps the children watched it happen, then they went out and found a few berries in the forest, other children and a road leading down to the coast, maybe a farmer to give them a ride. Hordes of children had come into the town that summer, diminutive, dusty beggars who crept in through cracks in doors and took a stubborn hold.

That had been ten years ago. Now Maret slept in the little room behind the kitchen, where she sang sad songs in a happy, piercing voice, as she curled her hair in the evenings with the aid of an old nail she had heated on the hob. In the mornings she would put on her white cap and arrange it so that a colourless little frizz of hair framed her cheeks, making her plain, empty face look like a pool edged with weeds; and then she would set off with her basket on her arm, full of expectation as if that day, of all days, was the day a wonderful promise would be fulfilled.

And Tobias went about stooped like an old man, keeping close to the walls of the house and looking down at the stones, the snow, the puddles, the blades of grass that made up his daily walk between the kitchen and the back door of the shop. Sometimes he would stop; on summer evenings he might even remove his spectacles and clean them and listen for a moment to the bright whistlings of the swallows and breathe in the scent of the bird cherry that grew by the barn, but he never varied his route, for he wanted nothing better than the familiar path where he would not go astray, the door that always stood open to him, the steaming kitchen with its pervasive cabbage smells, the chair he pulled up so close to the tiled stove that his face shone like the setting sun, and lastly the little garret where he had his bed and his window with the view over the neighbour's dungheap. He retired up there early each evening. Elisa said he was reading, but Jakob was pretty sure that he slept a lot, and that he went to sleep with the same sense of relief as other people wake up to find night is over and it is morning.

Jakob looked at the house where he had lived all his life. It was full of pathetic people. He no longer knew why he had come, whether it was to go inside for a little while, to stay for good or just to stand behind the barrels and watch. If he had been driven by homesickness, it was long since gone.

Nor did he need to go inside to know what they were doing, those pathetic people who had become his by pure chance and whom he accepted in the same way as he accepted no longer being able to run: Maret was taking the cooking pot from the stove, Tobias was puffing as he climbed the stairs, Lars Björnson was shutting his book and putting it under his arm and Elisa was slinging a pile of plates on to a table stained with grease and spilt beer.

He saw a trembling candle being carried from the kitchen up through the stairwell. Now Maret was putting the pot on the table. Tobias, who asked no more than to sit each evening with his back to the fire and silently eat turnips cooked to mush in salty stock, was chewing joylessly and mechanically; Maret was eating with the same delight as she did everything else and looking round for praise. Lars was reading his book. Elisa was gazing out of the window or rolling her serviette in her lap or drinking a glass of wine; she was bending over the food and staring at it as if it were coffee grounds or cards laid out for fortune telling, but when

Maret took the plate away she would go on staring at the table in the same way, or at the wall, or at the face of the person she was talking to.

That was how she had looked at him, like something to be divined. She had carried on in spite of all her disappointments, as if she were on the verge of a great revelation and could not relinquish the thought that there must be a meaning, a message, something in him that was much better, much nobler than what she could actually see.

When he was standing in the apothecary's shop in the daytime he could hear her pacing to and fro up there, to and fro between the window and the door of her narrow room. It was a room altogether too small for restlessness of such magnitude. He could hear the hard footfalls, the sound of a little table being knocked aside, the sound of a book being thrown to the floor, then a short pause: that meant she was standing at the window, gazing out. Sometimes it was quiet for so long he was obliged to go to the door to see whether anything had happened out in the street, but it never had. And soon it began again, the footfalls and the pauses in a regular rhythm which had been an accompaniment to his days for many years and to which he had grown accustomed in the same way you might grow accustomed to a loudly ticking clock, until at last you no longer hear it at all. Perhaps it had been wrong of him to grow accustomed, but that was the way out he had chosen. He was trying the alternative way out now. He did not think there was a third solution.

But there must have been a time when he did, since he had occasionally gone up to her room during the day and sat for a while on the bench by the window. He had thought that would suffice as proof of goodwill. It was always close in the room, but if he ever tried to touch her, her skin was ice cold, for it was only her anger that was hot. He had never known why she was so angry, nor with whom, but it had eventually seemed natural to assume it was himself. That had made everything much easier. He had pushed her away like a dish that did not agree with him; it made no difference if others praised it, since it made him ill.

It was even colder now. If he leant over the barrels he could see the moon in the bird cherry, a pale winter moon with a misty halo of frost. In there they had no doubt finished eating and sat down by the fire as they always did, as still and silent as the winter night with its thousand white stars whose names he had learnt and forgotten. It was easy to forget. Nor could he remember any of what had happened to himself and Elisa when they were really young, only that it had all come to an end. He had gone off to that war. Later he returned and was changed, with a shattered kneecap as a memento of his first and only campaign, and she changed too, although it did not show in the way she walked. He did not think the change in her had anything to do with him, it was the fault of time, time that changes everything into something else and that may, if you have the patience to wait, turn it back again.

Or maybe not, he did not know. He did not want to yearn for something that was gone for ever. And although the house was his, he did not miss it, for now he need never again go into her room and feel he was disturbing her while she was preoccupied with something he could not see. He did not know what it was, but he felt it, as resistance. It incensed him, for he had never asked anything of her.

Round them floated paper and glasses and rubbish and dirty clothes. Maret boiled the meat to stringy white fibres and Elisa sat wrapped in a blanket, reading and letting the fire go out. When the wick burnt down she sat in the dark. When the supply of candles was gone, their light came from a dish of smoky, reeking whale oil. But one quickly grows used to managing without everything that is comfortable, well arranged or just pleasant to the eye, and Jakob soon learnt to eat without thinking and to go to bed early to keep warm; to move as little as possible, to balance on a broken chair and drink from a dirty cup.

While Maret loitered at the front gate smiling at passers-by all day, Tobias went about coughing from the dust in the drying loft. With his crooked back, poor sight, scared voice and a paper-thin skull beneath his sparse hair, he was like a little dry root in the dead forest of birch leaves, hops, yarrow and camomile. Jakob had never said a harsh word to either of them. Sometimes he thought it was perhaps not Maret's extreme stupidity that made her draw two eyebrows on her forehead with a bit of charcoal before she expectantly set out for a walk, but that this was instead evidence of almost heroic courage. Yet sometimes he would also look around him at the table and say: 'A pretty pair of children we've got.'

The fact that Lars Björnson had been taken into Elisa's capricious care and been permitted to move into one of the attic rooms had not changed much; the only difference was that there were now two of them sitting mute before the fire reading instead of one. Lars did copying work at night and lived on coffee and bread, and once he had sold all his books he borrowed Elisa's. Sometimes they sat together and shared a single book; whoever reached the end of the page first would clear their throat and sometimes one would point out something that made the other nod, or laugh soundlessly. They were like two cats lapping from the same saucer.

Himself, he had increasingly taken to spending his evenings and nights down in the shop.

Then the children in the cellar came. Jakob knew that Maret would never be able to grasp the connection between the sounds you make with your mouth and lines you draw on a piece of paper, but Elisa had been trying to teach her to read for years. At regular intervals came those urgent outbursts of restless activity in which Maret's specially scrubbed fingers were made to form an 'o', which became a square, a triangle, a snake that slithered off across the table and vanished. 'Are you an idiot?' asked Elisa, grabbing the girl's hand which, transformed into a club or a tree branch, drew an 'o' that filled the whole room like a cloud or shrank to a pinpoint, an embryonic 'o' the size of an ant's egg. 'Good God, how stupid can the girl be?' shouted Elisa, and slammed the door as Maret began to howl. It was at this point that the children in the cellar arrived.

There were fourteen of them, for there was no space for more, seven girls and seven boys who were fed on gruel and lessons in reading, writing and something Lars Björnson called worldly wisdom, several times a week. Seated on blocks of wood, they wrote their names with sticks in the sand on the floor, added up empty medicine bottles and listened to stories about wise tortoises and emperors who got a taste of their own medicine. On Saturdays they got sandwiches with their gruel.

It was hard to tell what Lars Björnson felt, for he was like a broken instrument. If you touched the strings, no sound came, but much later a note might suddenly begin to echo in the slight stirring of the air as someone passed. Anyone wanting to know how much he missed his brothers had to look at the blots in the Mayor's record books or go to the little room where he sat writing at night with his back pressed up against the chimney wall he shared with Tobias.

He never spoke of the boys. He had brought them up, but when they disappeared he gave up everything that had belonged to them and was no longer needed: the rooms where they had grown up, the work that had put their food on the table. When all the money was gone, he was unmoved as he exchanged his own chair for a borrowed chair and read a borrowed book, for a chair is a chair, a book a book, regardless of who owns it. He copied records and wrote out contracts just as before, but now he did it in the attic instead of at the town hall and for a third of what he had been paid before. His fingers were still blue with ink.

In the evening he went down to the river and found fourteen lice-infested children playing with a dead cat, some stones and a bit of mud, which they were turning into a city surrounded by battlements; he took them home and taught them to write their names in the sand, and the children stared at symbols that were themselves, silent and in intense concentration as if they were searching for faces in the collections of circles and lines. He kept quiet so as not to frighten them. When he went round correcting what they had written, his hand sometimes rested a moment on a dirty head, as if by accident, as if for support. Anyone who wanted to know how much he loved his brothers would have to go down and see the children in the cellar.

The boys had both been blond, very like each other though one had not grown so tall. Only if he made a great effort could Jakob recall a faceless double silhouette. He seldom spoke to Lars. He had pinned up an old blanket over the window of Lars's room to keep out the draught, but he did not know if it helped, any more than had the candle he used to leave by Tobias's bed when the boy was little and had nightmares. Sometimes he sent Maret with a tray of broken sugar fish for the children downstairs, but he stayed where he was, for the house was finished now.

It was big, big enough to hold an apothecary's shop, a secret school, a writing desk overflowing with closely written sheets of paper and other things of which he knew nothing. It was full of pathetic people trying to guide each other and he thought this was as it should be. He only wished he had had more to give them. Perhaps it was his way of getting away, letting himself be stabbed in the arm, and perhaps Elisa had changed, now that the tremendous energy she had never known what to do with had finally found an outlet. Lars would try to teach her that you can make yourself understood by other means, but for himself he almost preferred the wound, because it was clear and simple. It was red and white, like the gaping jaws of an animal.

He rested his head on the fence and looked up at the grey façade of the house one last time. In the little room under the roof, a light was moving as Tobias came up to bed. Jakob could briefly see him standing at the window before a shadowy hand against the pale wallpaper reached out and smothered the wick. A creaking bolt was shot across the kitchen door, a piercing voice scared away the dark with a song about knights and maidens. In the bird cherry the moon sailed at amazing speed through the branches, out towards the sea.

The darkness was a black wing beating over the rooftops and he was a shadow on the snow. On the upper floor, two people bent their heads close together over something that rendered them blind to every movement out in the courtyard. There was a light in the window, it would burn all night. He opened the gate to the street and went home.

CHAPTER 4

He had slept for a couple of hours when Mattias Bredberg appeared at the warehouse door with a lantern in his hand and a fur over his arm, and said: 'The King's coming. And we're going out to meet him.' He threw the fur down on the bunk and sat himself on the table beside a piece of pork on a plate, then looked about him and said irritably: 'You have a hellish cold time of it here.'

Jakob knew the King had already come. After all, he could see him, on an ice-blue road, shoeless and with his uniform full of holes. 'It's his heart,' he mumbled, 'a bullet straight through the heart.'

'Not at all,' said Mattias, 'you know very well it got him in the head.'

'Yes,' said Jakob, and slipped further into a dream about a great, shaggy beast lying on top of his chest. He was conscious of Mattias being in the room and wanting something, but he would have to drive away the beast before he could get up. Straight in the head, he thought, and threw out his arms as if he were swimming, which seemed to help, because the beast ran off and he was on his way up, back to the room he had recently left, which looked big and strange in the lantern light. Sleep-dazed, he threw off the quilt and the fur and swung his legs over the side of the bunk.

55

Mattias picked up a knife, speared a bit of pork and put it in his mouth. 'Anyway,' he said, wiping the blade on his trouser leg, 'better in the head than in the back. Yet it's an odd way for a king to die, don't you think? Behind the line of fire. But he's dead, all the same, and if you've got any more of this pig hidden away somewhere, I should put it under lock and key, because they'll be here soon. And then all hell will break loose.'

'You're talking a load of rubbish,' said Jakob, rubbing his forehead. 'Who's coming? I haven't got any damned pig.'

'Oh yes you have, at home. But not for much longer, I promise you. Out into the forest with your little piggy, if you want to keep it.'

He turned the chair back to front and sat down on it with his arms folded along the top and his powerful legs wide apart. 'Now listen to me,' he said gravely, 'yesterday I said I didn't like the look of what I'd seen, but that was putting it extremely mildly. I think you ought to go home and set your house in order.'

'I was there a little while ago,' said Jakob, 'and it looked fine.'

'You're a bit dense, aren't you? Don't you realise the troops are on the homeward march and this is where they'll stop en route, and they'll be needing food and blankets and fuel and medicine and somewhere to sleep? We shall give them what they need, like we always do; it's just that this time it's going to be much worse than ever before.'

'Why?' asked Jakob sleepily.

'Because they've had a thrashing.'

He leant back a little and the lamplight transformed his face into an inflated, eyeless mask. 'They won't be asking permission when they get here,' he said with a smile. 'But perhaps you don't think this is any of your business?'

'I don't think it's any of your business who defends my house.'

'You can't be thinking Lars Björnson would frighten anybody?' said Mattias. 'With his violet eyes, good grief; they used to give me the shudders whenever he came into the room. Eyes like a girl. Or a kitten. And hands with hardly the strength to lift a pen.'

'I was thinking more of Elisa. I mean, she's got plenty of fight in her.'

'Her! She'll invite them to dinner just to provoke you. And bring up all the wine from the cellar, and kill the pig.'

'You can't know that for sure. She's just as likely to bar the door and sit reading with her fingers in her ears.'

'Yes, and let them kill the pig themselves. But it's a long time until spring, remember that, a long time until the ice melts and anything can grow in the soil.'

'What I think,' said Jakob, 'is that she won't do anything at all. In that way we're alike, at any rate.'

He got to his feet. Lack of food and sleep had left him feeling as light as a dried seed pod. He stretched so all his joints cracked and picked up the fur from the floor. 'Is this for me?' he asked, holding it up in front of him.

'Yes, it's for you,' said Mattias. 'So you don't get cold while we're waiting.'

He pushed the chair aside and put the fur carefully round Jakob's shoulders, which sagged a little under the weight. Then he said: 'What actually happened? Can't you tell me now?'

'I told her the King was dead and she stabbed me in the arm.'

'You must have said something to make her lose her temper?'

'I swear by God that's all that happened! The King's been shot, I said, and she reacted as if I'd fired the gun myself.'

'Hm,' said Mattias. 'You should never have let that notary into the house.'

'What was I supposed to do with him, then? You know him, you know how defenceless he is.'

'So others have to defend him instead. I could have had him indicted for high treason ten times over after all the things I've heard him say, out loud, the most unheard of things, and he hadn't even the wits to keep his voice down. I couldn't have kept him on even if he'd been my own brother, but as it so happens I can't stand the fellow. He's an irritant.'

'Some people think so.'

'He scared me, actually,' said Mattias, 'though I never let it show.'

'Rest assured he knew it all the same.'

'A person like that –'

'He's my friend,' Jakob interrupted him. 'And you can't leave a kitten out in the street just because it scratches.'

'But if you bring it in you have to expect fleas in your bed! Because, Elisa . . . well, she's always been a bit strange. And it hardly helped matters letting someone add fuel to the fire. Someone like that, who does nothing but puff away and talk rubbish, of course it flares up! But he's useless with the poker, that's one comfort.'

'Can't you shut up for a bit?' said Jakob, groping for the armhole. 'There's nothing wrong with either of them. Nor with you, come to that; you took me in off the street last night, after all, even though I was drunk and filthy. What do you think people are saying about that?'

'Well,' said Mattias, 'I expect they're saying what I'm thinking, that it mustn't become a habit. Once is all right, it's proof of friendship. The second time you do it out of Christian charity, but if it happens too often you end up looking stupid and gullible, and I'm not going to lay myself open to that, even for your sake.'

'Oh, people are saying a lot more than that,' said Jakob. 'But I don't give a damn what people say.'

He made a few circuits of the lantern, feeling the warmth spread though his body. Mattias had sat down again; he was carving at the chair back with the knife and appeared to be thinking of all the difficulties that lay ahead of them. He had a deep furrow between his brows and the same expression as when he was adding long columns of figures and forcing them to tally with the total. 'The spinning mill,' he muttered, 'there's plenty of space there. We'll have to use the spinning mill to start with.'

'What is it we're actually going to do?' asked Jakob in confusion.

'I thought you knew that. We're going out to meet the corpse.'

For the second time that evening, Jakob was obliged to put on his shoes and leave the safe, dusty darkness between the wood stacks. When he stepped out on to the loading platform, he noticed that the air was warmer and the moon had disappeared. There's more snow coming, he thought gloomily, and looked up at the sky. Which is worse for the men, intense cold or blocked roads? He tried to decide which he would opt for himself as Mattias went ahead with the lantern, whistling.

Mattias walked fast and blew out great clouds of white breath, as exhilarated as if they had been on their way to a party instead of a vigil over a dead body. The little tune sounded indecently cheerful as it bounced back and forth between the rows of warehouses and the cargo boats frozen into the ice. 'The notary would have liked to be the one holding the gun, that's for certain,' he called over his shoulder. 'Even small people can be dangerous.' It was as if he had already forgotten all the problems that lay ahead of them, or as if he was looking forward to solving them.

Jakob looked at the broad back, the thick neck and the fur-hatted head bobbing along in front of him. 'You're quite small yourself,' he said quietly.

'Surely you're not implying I'm dangerous?'

'Well, Leo Fahlgren seems to think so, at any rate. Why else would he send his son to spy on you?'

'Oh, him. He thinks I hide smuggled goods in my bales of tobacco, and now he wants a share in the profits.'

'Do you?' asked Jakob. 'Smuggle, I mean.'

'Of course,' said Mattias, swinging his arm and sending a beam of light sweeping out over the water, which ran sluggish and turbid through an ice-edged channel. 'But if I'm going to take all the risk, I want all the profit too. Leo can get his own boats.'

He stopped, set down the lantern on a bollard and took his pipe out of his coat pocket. 'Ideally, I'd like to be rid of them altogether,' he said thoughtfully, 'cautious Leo and his son who asks all the questions. Then you and I could go into partnership instead; you could run the day-to-day business so I had more time for other things, we'd both profit by it. I'd lend you some money to get started.'

'You've said that before. But I don't want to.'

'Why not, though?' said Mattias in annoyance. 'Why would anyone want to be badly off when they could be well off?'

'It's hard to explain.'

Mattias lit his pipe from the lantern and puffed in silence. 'And anyway, I'm not badly off,' said Jakob.

In the town above them, a fire suddenly flared between the solid shapes of the houses and some dark figures hurried by, cowering from the shower of sparks. 'See?' said Mattias, pointing with his pipe. 'They're on the move.' A dog barked in a hoarse monotone until it woke other dogs and the barking ran like a chain through the town, but apart from that the anxiety up there was soundless. The houses still lay in darkness. Jakob thought of the people standing at the windows and looking out on to the streets, where the occasional fur-clad figure might be passing, but where otherwise it was as peaceful as any ordinary evening.

'Myself, I've hardly slept a wink this past week,' said Mattias. 'When the word came I was dressed and ready, all the preparations were made. We're to meet on the north edge of town.'

'We'd better go then, hadn't we?' asked Jakob, but Mattias gave no reply. He sucked on his pipe and leant his head against the wall of a ramshackle warehouse with a strong smell of herring.

'Not yet,' he said slowly. 'It's nice here, it's so quiet. It's hard to imagine how noisy it is here each spring with everybody running about and all the boats and the barrels to be rolled on board and goods to be loaded on to carts.' He took a flask of schnapps out of his pocket and drank a deep draught before handing the flask to Jakob. 'Every moment there are questions to be answered and things to be decided . . .'

'And there are probably times when you get tired of it all,' said Jakob, tipping back his head to drink.

They stood silent for a moment, feeling the effect of the spirits, and looked out to the invisible sea which breathed over them with its strong, cold mouth. Then Mattias knocked the ash out of his pipe and said: 'What are you thinking of doing now?'

'Now?' said Jakob. 'Aren't I coming with you? Isn't that why you came to fetch me?'

'I mean afterwards. What will you do afterwards?'

'I don't know,' said Jakob. 'Stay in the warehouse, I suppose. When spring comes I can hire a boat or buy a bit of land. You did say you could lend me some money, after all.' He was still listening out for the sea, which was impossible to hear and yet was sighing with the same sound as the blood in your ears when you have a fever, soft and unvoiced.

'I don't invest money in hopeless ventures,' said Mattias. 'I've nothing against a bit of risk, but there's got to be some shred of a chance of profit. And you're no farmer, I don't know what you are. Wessman's an old fool, but what he said yesterday was right: your father left you a first-rate little plot and you've done your best to ruin it. You can't just let things carry on the way they always have when you're running a business, you have to keep up with the times. And if you're not suited to the work, you have to let somebody else take over.'

'But that's just what I *have* done,' said Jakob, but Mattias wasn't listening. 'We merchants have got to stick together,' he yelled, kicking a lump of snow out in a wide arc over the water. 'I've never known worse times, and now we've no king either, and no heir to the throne, it's too damned bad. What a racket those rats are going to make as they fight over the cheese! But if they take our trading rights away from us again, we might as well put up the shutters in this town.'

'It can't possibly depend on how many cough lozenges I sell in my shop, though,' said Jakob, trying not to laugh.

'Oh yes it can! Because you don't keep faith like the rest of us. You're no credit to your class.'

He thrust his pipe into his pocket and reached for the lantern, which had sunk sideways into a pile of half-melted snow. As he held it straight and the flame burnt up, Jakob could see that he wasn't angry as he'd thought, but sad, sad the way he had been when they were little and someone spoilt the game, tapped his foot out of time, sang the verses in the wrong order and eventually broke the circle with a roar of laughter that carried the other children with him. It had hurt Mattias that they would rather run around the yard shrieking and chasing one another.

'Come on,' said Jakob, putting his hand on the back turned on him, just as he used to do in the old days, 'let's go, so we don't get there too late.'

'If we lose our rights as a trading centre I'll be forced to go over to fishing,' said Mattias. 'Or I shall have to move to Gothenburg.'

'Come on,' said Jakob, and pushed him on ahead towards the ramp that ran from the last warehouse to the beach below.

This time, he was the one carrying the lantern. The path he had worn as he tramped back and forth to the town was not wide enough for two, so he let Mattias go first and held the lantern high to stop him stumbling over the frozen cart tracks under the snow. They followed the river all the way up to the iron bridge and paused for a moment outside the town hall, where the door was open and they could see people scurrying around inside, unfolding black cloth and strewing the floor with chopped fir twigs.

Mattias gave a 'hmm', then stuck his hands in his pockets and moved on. Jakob had been thinking of going in to ask the time, but it was either very late or very early and he contented himself with that. Now it was his route they were following, the road leading north. It narrowed as the houses grew smaller, and each spring, rain and cattle hooves turned it into a muddy ditch. It ran alongside gardens and came out on the common, where the troops had pitched camp on their way to Norway in the summer. Fires had burnt there then, and the cows had fled and hidden in the fringes of the forest. Now there was a cold wind blowing from the wide meadows, and when they reached the spinning mill Mattias stood for quite some time regarding the building, as if trying to work out how many sleeping places it could accommodate.

They had seen no one else on the way, but when they emerged at the north edge of town they found that everybody was already there, some fifty townsmen dressed in black, holding unlit torches, stamping round in circles and drinking from little flasks. Some of them were busy dragging firewood from the forest and a man with a lantern had climbed a slight rise at the other end of the common, from where there was a better view of the road into town. 'No-o,' he called from his vantage point, 'I can't see anything.' His voice sounded muffled, as if he were talking through cotton wool.

In the centre, where a bonfire was being built, Leo Fahlgren sat on a chair brought along for the purpose. 'Look, the Mayor's here now,' he cried, and brandished his stick, 'so it's only the King we're still waiting for. Superior people always arrive late.'

'Oh, the King's on his way,' said someone. 'He's got no choice, poor fellow.'

'Well, nor have we, for that matter,' said someone else. 'Because if we had, I should have stayed in my bed. It's going to snow any minute, just you see.'

'And look who he's got with him,' said Leo as the straw beneath the kindling ignited, illuminating the faces bending over it. 'The troublemaker. It's lucky Wessman couldn't come.'

'Ah yes,' said somebody, and laughed, 'that's right, he couldn't come.'

Jakob took a swig from Mattias's flask and held out his numb hands to the fire. 'Is Wessman ill?' he asked.

'Would that be so surprising?' said the Dean. 'After the rough treatment he had from you last night?'

'Wessman suffers from an acid stomach,' said the ruddy doctor, elbowing aside an insignificant postal official to get nearer the fire. 'It's a complaint that can be extremely uncomfortable, but one seldom dies of it.'

'And what does the doctor recommend?'

'A cup of camomile tea usually eases it.'

'Poor Wessman, he'll have to go to the apothecary!'

'I'll send the boy round with a bagful tomorrow,' said Jakob. He did not remember much of the evening before, only that he had done something he regretted.

The man with the lantern came trudging towards them, his hair glittering with frost. 'The air's as thick as gruel,' he said, 'you can't hear or see a thing.' A pimply youth tried to get through to the fire with some branches of oak, but Fahlgren lashed out in his direction with his stick and cried: 'No, no, you must know those won't burn? Put them aside to dry out first.' Then he folded his hands on the crook of

65

the stick and asked: 'And what has the Mayor been up to? The rest of us have been waiting almost an hour.'

'I've been considering where we can accommodate our guests,' said Mattias.

He had taken off his cap and run his fingers through his thick, sandy hair. His face, so much younger than the other men's, softened in the light from the blazing fire; his eyes narrowed as though not even he could resist the temptations of the warmth: to stop, to fall silent, to rest, to sleep. He had been up too long but Jakob, who could feel the arm that was pressed against his own quivering with eagerness and irritation, was not surprised when Mattias turned away from the fire with an impatient jerk and said: 'Two hundred in the spinning mill, that's all there's room for. The doctor will have to answer for the hospital himself.'

'But wait a moment, my dear boy,' said Leo Fahlgren. He looked round with satisfaction at the other men, who were all sick and tired of being frozen and anxious and muttered sleepily that they had quite enough to cope with as it was. 'Surely there's no need to meet trouble halfway?' he went on. 'And surely we can't evacuate the whole town on the strength of a few stray rumours?'

'You are an old fool,' said Mattias softly.

'An old fool who's seen his fair share of the world, yes!'

'Fools don't see the world, they only see themselves. We've all looked after our own interests, and in good times that's a good principle. But in a few days we'll have the soldiers here, and whether we want to or not, we'll be obliged to take them in.'

A slow wave of resignation seemed to wash through the men who were crowded round the fire in close circles. 'But who will bear the cost?' asked someone cautiously. From

66

behind him came a laugh, hoarse as a coughing fit. 'Fifty beds,' said the doctor, 'I can't promise more. But it's essential that we reserve them for those needing treatment.'

'And why should anybody need treatment?' cried the retired Colonel who had hitched a lift with the wagon bringing the wood, and was rosy and rested. 'Just because our army happens to have retreated a few dozen kilometres for the time being, it doesn't mean the men need to go straight to bed, does it?'

'We must prepare for the worst,' said Mattias patiently, kicking at a glowing brand that had rolled out of the fire. 'Hey, more wood here!' he called, and the pimply youth who had been banished from the warmth pushed his way through the circle with a shrubby juniper, catching Leo Fahlgren on the ear with it as he passed. Everyone fell silent for a moment, hypnotised by the fire as it fizzed and crackled, sending up a cascade of glowing needles against the night sky, then Mattias pulled on his cap and said: 'If we wait any longer it'll be too late.'

'It's always a good idea to look ahead,' said Leo Fahlgren. 'Look at me, I've had a consignment of black baize lying in my store for years, and it'll come in very handy now the church is to be clad for mourning. You have to let your business deals mature before you reap the rewards.'

'Perhaps you shouldn't think of your business deals all the time,' said the Dean.

'That really is the limit, considering I've got two ambassadors lodging with me! They spend their time clucking and laying new dispatches every quarter of an hour. Who can run a business under those conditions?'

'They say the royal family is staying at one of the larger houses outside town,' said someone.

'And we've got a whole houseful of officers.'

'We shall all be obliged to open our homes,' said Mattias. 'Though it won't be a matter of courtiers and officers, but of several thousand soldiers who won't find places anywhere.'

'We must consider the possibility of an epidemic, of course,' said the doctor. 'It's happened before.'

At the word epidemic, the flasks all came out again. They circulated and were gradually drained as the snow of which everyone had spoken began to fall in thick, wet flakes that stuck to hair and clothes and made the horse, still harnessed to the wagon, whinny sadly beneath its blanket. Jakob did not hear the horse, nor the men's concerned talk, nor the fizzing of the damp wood; he stood there inside his fur as if in a well-heated house, listening to the snow. The sound was softer than a whisper, dry as the rustle of an abandoned book with its pages turned by the wind. It sounded like ants in a forest in summer.

'The King's coming!' shouted the man with the lantern. They all turned and looked towards the brow of the hill, over which the black caravan came snaking. 'Oh my Lord and Maker,' said a trembling old voice beside Jakob. 'The King truly is coming.'

All they could see was a shapeless mass flanked by a few isolated torches shining dully through the sleety snow, but a couple of the men took off their hats and the Dean pulled his hymn book of out of his pocket and cleared his throat. 'We must go and meet them, of course,' said Mattias crossly. 'Put your hats back on so you don't make yourselves ill, light the torches and move the wagon out of the way; it's blocking the whole place! You come with me, sir.' The old Colonel stared with red-rimmed eyes at the procession of mourners and held out a shaking hand for Mattias to grasp.

Behind them, the fire was flaring up from the last of the firewood. The men who had just now seemed so ponderous and heavy-hearted ran about nervously, jostling each other as they tried to get through to light their torches. The only one who did not move was Leo Fahlgren. 'We should have brought a few potatoes,' he announced, poking the embers with his stick. His son had climbed on to the back of the wagon to see better, and when the horse felt the motion it gave a low, guttural, gurgling sound. From the other side of the common, another horse answered equally dejectedly, and then they could see the cart being drawn at the head of the procession beneath a flag that refused to flutter in the damp air and hung as slack and heavy as a sack.

'Start walking,' shouted Mattias, and pulled the Colonel with him out into the wagon tracks that were fast disappearing under new snow. The Dean followed close behind with the senior aldermen, and behind them all the others in a bunch. Some tried to adopt a marching pace, but most of them trudged on as usual, blinking in the snow and holding their torches out sideways so as not to burn anybody with them. 'Hold them up, then!' barked Hans Fahlgren from the group at the rear, and at once the torches were held aloft, some fifty bobbing points of light in the grey-streaked darkness.

But Jakob stayed where he was. He stood by the fire that had almost burnt itself out, finished the contents of the flask and listened for the vague sound of jangling weapons and creaking wood carried on the wind. Then he walked over to the edge of the forest and watched the two groups marching towards each other, the long file of soldiers and the little knot of cautious men slipping in the wet snow. He saw the townsmen take off their hats and caps and raise their torches high so the light fell on the horses, the cart, the coffin and the gold-emblazoned rapiers in the hands of the guards; he heard someone speak, fragments of a prayer. Then the whole group was in motion again, the procession of torch-bearers dividing itself clumsily to either side of the cart, which was making swifter progress on the well-worn ground. Jakob positioned himself behind a tree and watched the procession of soldiers continuing to pour over the crest of the hill and on past him to disappear into the town.

He stood there for some considerable time. Finally he followed the men, walking slowly to keep a distance between himself and them. The dull tramp of two hundred and fifty pairs of feet was still echoing between the houses. As he approached the square he could see that the townspeople had begun issuing from their doorways, and in front of the town hall there was already a small gathering looking at the empty cart, at the horses hanging over their nosebags and the soldiers who had fallen asleep leaning against house walls or huddled up against each other. This was what they had all been fearing through the long autumn months, this sound of marching feet, this very sight: the exhausted, defeated men. The rumours had heralded their arrival and, now they were here, the bad times. Now it was no longer enough to lock your front door and go to bed early to save candles.

The buildings on both sides of the square were gleaming in the light from the torches, which had been thrown down in a heap and covered with debris from back courtyards, and in every little window people could be seen crowding to look out. Some of the ragged children from the straw huts chased one another shrieking round the bonfire, while two much older boys lunged for them with broken-off bits of planking and shouted to them to be quiet. There was light

70

in the town hall and the doors were open so Jakob, who had stopped by the doctor's fence, could see straight into the main hall, where blue-uniformed Life Guards and black-clad townsmen were thronging around the coffin, now placed on a table. Two candelabra, each as tall as a man, had been set on either side of the catafalque, but the draught from the door as people came and went kept blowing out the candles, and an anxious old servant made his way back and forth with a tarred taper, trying to light them again.

All at once, a closed carriage with a crown painted on the door drew up outside, a man got out and helped a woman in voluminous skirts to descend. They went into the town hall and the door closed. The crowd was growing all the time; men and women awoken by all the commotion were pacing uneasily to and fro across the open space or standing at the foot of the steps as if waiting for something: a declaration, a drum roll, an announcement about the future, a fanfare. A dog that had got sparks in its coat ran howling between their feet and hid under the cart. An old woman went about distributing wrinkled apples from a basket, another took round a jug of beer. From the town hall came the sound of a hymn being sung, and some of those in the square tentatively joined in while others made a great show of moving away. They went and stood by the fire instead, threw in any bits of wood that were still lying around or talked anxiously to some neighbour. Close by sat a group of soldiers, hunched up on their knapsacks, warming themselves.

Jakob could see them very clearly from his hiding place in the doctor's gateway. Someone threw a smashed herring barrel on to the fire and the blaze lit up their tired faces, the grey lips, the cheeks glistening with week-old stubble. The brims of their hats were shaggy with snow, their thin

71

stockings as yellow as butter in summer. Some were drinking from wooden tankards and talking quietly among themselves, others were asleep, heads slumping. One had taken off a shoe and was trying to mend it with a short length of string. Most of them were young, but there were also a few older men among them, with lined faces and grey pigtails dangling over the collars of their coats. They all seemed at peace, unperturbed by the yelling children and the people crowding round the fire.

He went a little closer and tried to make out what they were saying, but all he could hear was a low, monotone growl. They were sitting quite motionless in the midst of the swelling alarm. The townspeople, who had never been on a battle-field and knew no more of war than the tales they had been told, went nervously tramping and parading past, round and round in small columns; they felt obliged to keep on the move, to talk, ask questions, wait for answers, listen out for news; but the rumours of catastrophe preoccupying them seemed for the moment no concern of these tired men. They already knew, or they knew nothing. They threw bits of wood on the fire, laughed and chewed hungrily on hard bread.

He was aware of their smell, a raw yet strangely clean smell of sweat and gunpowder. The hands clasping the tankards were brown. The uniforms were clean and neat although they were scarcely thick enough to keep out the cold. He could see now that all their shoes were worn through.

He thought he might be able to exchange a few words with them, to pat one of those bent backs and ask some-thing; nothing special, nothing about the state of the weather or the outcome of the war, just something to prompt an easy answer and give him a few minutes there at the fire with them. But as he took a step forward and stretched out

72

his hand, someone called his name, and when he turned round, he saw that the doors of the town hall were open and Mattias had come out on to the steps with a fat, white-haired old man.

They said something to each other and Mattias pointed to Jakob. Then they began slowly making their way across the square towards him.

CHAPTER 5

When Jakob emerged from the Mayor's house at about noon, he saw a woman pacing back and forth on the bridge as if waiting for someone. She had her hood up, hiding her face, but he recognised her walk, the long, slightly jerky strides. Taking no notice of the stream of people going past, the bunches of drunken soldiers, the officers holding their horses and leaving no way through for the carts from the countryside, she leant for a moment on the iron railing and watched the dirty water bubbling in its deep, ice-edged channel. She squeezed a handful of snow into a ball and threw it upriver, then turned abruptly and resumed her patrol. He knew who she was waiting for.

The night on the town hall square had already receded into something strange that had happened long ago. He had slept for a few hours and eaten breakfast while chatting to Sofie, who was cross because the royal secretary who had taken over the children's room had criticised the way the bed was made. No, she corrected herself, he hadn't exactly criticised, just pointed out that there were better ways of folding the corners of the sheets. The children had slept in her bed and the little boy had kicked all night, so she had ended up sleeping in a chair. What was more, she had been obliged to change her dress, and she claimed the smell of the black

74

material made her head ache. She didn't know where Mattias had slept, but he had long since gone out, in any case.

Jakob looked at the woman on the bridge. A soldier shouted something after her and she brushed off the words with the same mechanical movement you might use to flick away a troublesome fly. She would stand there all day if need be, letting herself be shoved and jostled by old women with loaded baskets, schoolboys on their Christmas holidays, harassed couriers with important messages, very important messages that were to be delivered immediately, and carts of rye barrels and squealing pigs. She was standing amid all the slush sprayed up by the cartwheels and waiting for him to come. Attempting to back into the building, he slipped on the steps, and then she saw him.

He thrust his hands into his pockets and went across to her, slowly, not raising his head until he was standing so close that he was obliged to. 'Out of the way, for God's sake!' came a shout, as a steaming horse ploughed across the bridge at an angle, kicking over a basket of swedes; and he took her by the arm and pulled her down on to the path which ran along by the river under a row of old elms. The trees were full of birds, chattering jackdaws that rose into the air at regular intervals and took a few aimless black turns over the rooftops before settling again; the ground beneath them was covered in droppings and torn-off twigs.

'Do you want to talk to me?' he asked.

'Don't want to,' she said. 'But I suppose I must.'

He had let go of her arm and they moved apart a little, dogged as two duelling partners on the way to their assignation. The population of the town had increased by a fifth in only a few days, but the further they went from the streets round the town hall, the more solitary they found

75

themselves. There was a roaring from the falls where Mattias had his sawmill and a rumble from the other mills; the slight thaw had turned the little river into a browny-yellow torrent with deep eddies and dirty foam, and round the trailing weeping willows, rafts of rubbish had accumulated, which worked themselves free whenever they got heavy enough and floated off under the bridges to be smashed to pieces. The pond at the base of the falls had grown into a lake, with high waves breaking against the retaining wall. They went to stand on the edge and looked at the water as it hurled itself down the rock face and then rose again, as smoke. Whenever the sun forced its way through the clouds, a little rainbow could be seen quivering in the watery haze.

For a few minutes they were almost friends, both absorbed in equally childlike fashion in the falls and the fruit-drop colours of the rays of light. Then Elisa threw back her hood and Jakob saw that she had not changed in the least, was still inaccessible behind her dark, angular face. She had a large mouth and he had always thought it rather attractive, but her brown eyes were a little too close together, which made her appear suspicious, even a little ill-natured. She wasn't ill-natured, he knew that, merely sensitive to injustices and quick to detect them. Her hair could have been attractive too, if only she hadn't worn it pulled back so severely.

In order to be able to talk, they were obliged to draw back from the falls and some way up the slope towards the church. He went and stood under an oak while she walked to and fro and looked about her as if she thought there were people among the trees, listening to them. 'I just wanted to know if you'd heard anything,' she said at last. 'Because you were there yesterday evening, I know that.'

'What ought I to have heard?' asked Jakob.

'Something about the boys, of course!'

'They're not in the King's Life Guards.'

She stopped and looked at him in confusion and he realised that, for her, there was no pattern to the events that were unfolding; for her, war was one endless file of soldiers on their way home. 'The Life Guards,' he tried to explain, 'they're just escorting the coffin. I don't know where Lars's brothers have got to, but they're not here.'

'But surely you might still have heard something about them.'

'I haven't heard anything and I haven't asked. There are thousands of men still up there, thousands. Who can I ask about two blond boys who disappeared from home last summer and haven't been heard of since?'

'I suppose I shall have to do it myself, then,' she said, but she did not go; she stood with her back to a tree trunk and stroked her red hand down her skirts, which were dirtied with muddy water.

'No, don't,' he said. 'They'll only laugh at you.'

Behind them, two men pushed a loaded cart up to the church, puffing and panting and swearing at the slush, the wind, the cracked wheels and the steepness of the hill. Jakob smiled at the coarse voices cursing life, and slipping into a much softer register as soon as the cart reached the top. He wished he could have found such a simple outlet for his own violent irritation at Elisa's way of shutting her mouth on the contemptuous words she thought he deserved, but did not consider worth speaking. For her, he was a stone lying in the road or a slow animal it was pointless to cajole; but he did not want to be seen as a stone or an animal when he felt like a leaf floating on the water, being whirled round in the eddies, something drifting and enjoying being adrift.

'Where can they be?' muttered Elisa, looking up at the naked black tops of the oak trees and the ragged clouds. 'Where can the boys have gone?' Jakob said nothing and shrugged his shoulders, at which she turned to him and screamed: 'You never know anything!'

He let go of the tree trunk and began picking his way carefully down the slippery incline, to where he would be able to see the river and the sailing gulls and the ducks patiently paddling against the current. Behind him, he heard the rough sound of her smoothing her hair with her hand, stroking and stroking as she tried to calm herself, and after a little while she came and stood beside him. 'How are things at home?' he asked her then, taking a sideways glance at the dark head with its shining white parting. 'All's well,' she said. Then they stood in silence, but he could tell she was thinking about something, trying to say something. He kicked at a lump of ice, looked at the birds and wished she would hurry up a bit.

'I've heard,' she said after a time, so quietly that he could hardly make out the words in the roar of the water, 'I've heard that lots of people are lost on the mountain.'

'I've heard that, too,' said Jakob.

'Is it true, then?' she said, and he was suddenly enraged by her questions, her demand that he should answer them, the way she clicked her tongue when he couldn't. 'I'm not in touch with the general staff, for Christ's sake!' he shouted. 'But what I do know is that if they're lost on the mountain they're in real trouble, because they're not dressed for it.'

'How can you know what they're wearing?' she said dismissively. 'You said yourself you don't know a thing.'

'But I've seen the soldiers. And they're in summer uniforms;

no warm coats, nothing proper on their hands. You don't get far on a mountain in clothes like that.'

'What are you talking about?' said Elisa, grabbing his arm.

'Clothes,' he said slowly. 'They've no warm clothes.'

'But why ever not? It's winter, isn't it?'

'It was summer when they set off. Everybody thought it would be a short campaign.'

'But surely you have to pack warm clothes, even so?' she said, shaking him. 'Surely you can't just forget it'll be cold when winter comes?'

'That sort of thing happens in war,' said Jakob, trying to shake off the hand that was pulling on his arm and making it throb. It was his bad arm, but she seemed to have forgotten the fact.

Suddenly she started to laugh. 'I don't believe you,' she yelled. 'You're making fun of me. It can't be true that they let the outcome of the war depend on the supply of wool.'

'The supply of wool, of fresh food, of shelter from the wind . . . The state of the roads, the weather, the fog risk; those things decide the outcome more often than people realise.'

'But it's absurd! When you think of how much work it takes to make a human being, to teach him to walk and talk and work and be capable of interesting conversation, surely they can't go and forget such a simple thing as packing properly?'

'It's impossible to predict everything.'

'But snow at this time of year, surely they can predict that? And the fact that people freeze when it's cold? Either the King's a fool or you're lying, and since everyone says the King's a military genius, you must be making it all up. And that means you might well be lying about the boys, too; perhaps they're here in town and you just couldn't be bothered to look for them.'

'Why should anybody need to look for them?' said Jakob wearily. 'They would have searched you out for themselves, wouldn't they? They're not in town.'

'So the King *is* a fool, after all,' she said spitefully. 'Did you know that? Though of course there's a third way of looking at it. If the King's *not* a fool and you're *not* lying about the uniforms, then it must mean nobody cares any longer whether people die. And if you've been warmongering for twenty years, maybe it doesn't matter how they die either, whether they get a bullet in the belly or just lie where they fall in a snowdrift. Maybe you get used to the losses and make allowance for them. Like what goes to waste at the sawmill.'

'But it's childish to think no one will get hurt,' said Jakob. 'That's what happens in war.'

'That people die,' she said. 'But what do they get for dying? And what do they get for not dying?'

'I don't understand what you mean,' said Jakob. 'You talk as if it was some sort of business deal.'

'Isn't it, then? The same as the sawmill?'

'What's the sawmill got to do with me? Stop going on about it, it's Mattias's sawmill.'

She started to laugh again, a sound like a puppy trying to bark. 'Yes, he would have organised it all much better,' she said, breathless and wiping her eyes. 'I saw him running around down there in his fur coat directing the carts and shouting at the hands who had forgotten to put fir twigs on the steps; he was sweating and shouting, he was happy. Because Mattias never gets taken by surprise, never gets caught napping, never takes unnecessary risks, buys everything at the lowest possible price and never makes a bad deal. He wouldn't forget to pack properly. And if it started snowing in the middle of summer he'd be ready for that, too.'

Jakob took hold of her and tried to make her stop laughing, at which she lashed out with her arm, scratching him on the back of the hand with her ring. When he saw the streak of blood he felt the same fury as before, a sharp, white fury that almost blinded him. He stumbled back, sat down in a snowdrift and shouted: 'Go to hell!'

'Go to hell yourself,' she said wearily, and suddenly applied herself to brushing her skirts with such energy that the dried mud came loose in big lumps. 'I've no use for you, either. Because you . . . you're one of those people who only ever looks on. From a distance. It was always like that, you never went close. You never looked properly; you were asleep. That was why you only understood half the things I said.'

'But now you're awake,' she went on angrily, and looked at him. 'It's very strange, but now you're awake!'

The sky had darkened as they talked, the wind was gusting and shaking lumps of snow down from the branches. It sounded as if there was someone walking in there under the trees with great, wet footsteps.

'I think you should come home,' said Elisa, spying nervously into the darkness of the hazel thicket as if searching for something.

'Nothing,' said Jakob, getting up, 'nothing in the whole world would make me come home ever again.'

'You needn't think it would be for my sake,' she said quickly. 'It's Lars who wants to see you.'

'Did he say so?'

'No,' she said. 'But I know he wants to see you. He's ill.'

'He's been ill for as long as I can remember.'

'Yes, but he's worse now. I think he's dying.'

Dying, thought Jakob.

He tried to imagine what it would mean if Lars died. He knew what death implied for himself, for he had touched it once a long time ago and still retained the memory of his own gratitude at being spared. He knew, too, how quickly the cold kills a human being already weakened by hunger and exhaustion, how easily it comes, how invisible it is. He could read the signs and foresee the outcome of what was going on around them now, and none of it surprised or shocked him because it is natural to die, whether it happens by means of a bullet or in a snowdrift. He could remember it, the thought, 'I'm going to die now,' and how self-evident it was. Death was white, it was blood red, sometimes it was a grey smoke that covered your eyes and made it hard to breathe, but it was always clearly obvious. The only thing he couldn't see was Lars Björnson's death, although that was more likely than any other and had been in preparation for so long.

'Give him what you usually do,' he said. 'I've nothing better to suggest.'

'He wants to see you,' she said.

'I'm not a doctor. Tell him to go to bed.'

'But he doesn't *want* to go to bed.'

She chewed her thumbnail and stared at him stubbornly. 'Is that why the pair of you sit up at night?' Jakob asked, but she didn't answer. 'What do you do at night?' he asked again. 'Why is the candle left burning? What is it you're writing in the middle of the night?' Elisa laughed and turned away.

He was glad he couldn't go home. He would escape doing what she asked, be prevented from sitting by a bed and measuring drops into a spoon; but as soon as he had thought the thought, he forgot what it was he was glad to escape and recalled only the task that had got in the way. He felt the rustle of paper in his trouser pocket and said, 'I've got to go.'

'Go where?' she said, and he took out the piece of paper and smoothed it flat as he thought about what he had written down during the night at the old doctor's dictation: *aqua apoplectica*, *gummi arabicum*, *lavendula spica* . . . hyssop, thyme, southernwood, spikenard, camomile . . . It ran to thirty-six items; it was a long list. 'I'm going to the town hall,' he said, holding it out to her. 'I've been asked to help the King's personal physician when the body's being prepared. Take this list and give it to Tobias, tell him to have it all ready for collection by five o'clock at the latest.'

'What's all this?' said Elisa, looking at the jottings covering the paper. 'What do you mean, when the body's being prepared?'

'It's to be embalmed so it survives the journey up to Stockholm.'

'The King's being salted down,' she said with a thoughtful nod; then she took the list and read through it again.

'Give it to Tobias,' Jakob said again, 'he knows exactly what –'

'You haven't been listening, have you?' she said, interrupting him with an abrupt gesture. 'Either that or you misunderstood what I told you just now. For surely you can't think it more important to pour perfume on a corpse than to help a friend who's ill? Of course you don't, nobody does. You can give Tobias the list yourself when you come back home with me.'

'I'm not going home,' said Jakob, 'I'm going to the town hall. I've more or less been ordered to go there and help.'

'Don't be ridiculous,' she said. 'They can't give you orders.'

'I've promised and I'm not going to break that promise.'

'You can break that promise, because it isn't worth anything. What you're going to do in the town hall isn't worth anything and that makes the promise just as worthless, just as dead as a half-rotten body. Bury it in the ground and come home with me.'

'I'm not going to do that,' said Jakob slowly. 'I'm going to the town hall, because that's what I most want to do.'

She took a step towards him, extended her hand, opened her mouth. He expected her to start screaming again or trying to drag him away, but she merely let go of the paper, which was whisked away by the wind and caught on a branch. With a curse he snatched it back and pressed it to his trouser leg to stop the water obliterating the writing; he waved it to and fro in the air to dry.

Elisa smiled at him. 'Go then,' she said calmly, 'and hurry up. Hurry up or you'll be late.' Then she turned and set off at a run along the riverside, head down with her hood inflated like a balloon, but on the steps up to the street she paused for a moment and called: 'We're thinking of not salting down the pig this year. We don't think we'll need to.'

At that moment, Jakob heard a crack behind him and a soft thud like someone dropping a sack of flour. He wheeled round and saw Leo Fahlgren lying on the edge of the trees with snow all over his face and a broken hazel branch in his hand. 'Help me, then,' called Leo. 'Surely you can see I can't move? It's dangerous lying on a cold surface when you're as old as I am.'

He must have leant over a little too far in his attempt to overhear what they were saying, but he did not seem remotely embarrassed at having been caught, merely slightly irritated by the wet patches on the knees of his trousers, which he rubbed at with a handkerchief as Jakob stood him upright and brushed off his coat. 'I was up in the church,' he explained, 'to see how the black baize was looking, and I decided to come back through the copse. Idiotic at my age, everyone knows how unsteady old fellows are. Like boats without keels. But what luck, my happening to fall down just here, exactly where you happened to be. Wasn't that lucky?'

'It certainly was,' said Jakob, looking over to the road where Elisa had disappeared out of sight.

'You and your delightful wife. It quite restores one's faith in the meaning of life.'

Jakob had nothing against Leo's babble, which was malicious but quite understandable. He retrieved the man's hat from the ground, set it back on his head, held out his arm and let Leo hook firmly on to it. 'Since you're on your way to the town hall, perhaps we can walk together for a bit,' said Leo, poking an explorative foot into the slush. 'I'd thought of looking in on my old friend Wessman on the way, and of course he lives right next door. Shall I give him your regards?'

'How did the black baize turn out?' asked Jakob, trying to accommodate his step to the old man's cautious shuffle up the slope.

'Excellently,' said Leo. 'I'm so glad I voted for the building of a new church, though it hit me hard in the purse.' He pulled Jakob to him and whispered: 'Piety pays. The new church is at least twice the size of the old one.'

Very slowly, with interruptions for Leo to catch his breath, mop his brow and beat the snow off the bushes with his stick, they toiled up the long set of steps to the street. 'Glorious weather,' said Leo, at the same instant as

85

a blue-black cloud opened over the church and sent down a shower of hailstones.

'I can't see anything glorious in weather like this,' said Jakob, trying to shield his head with his arm.

'You're right,' said Leo, 'it's detestable; cold and raw and blowing a gale. I go around thinking about women all the time, and that makes me talk a load of nonsense. It's beastly weather. As bad as in Gomorrah, though in its own way.

'Women,' he mused, once they had sought shelter beneath some eaves, 'women have no sense. Don't need any either, it only makes them nervous. The least little gleam of light penetrating a female skull is enough to cause misery to everyone around her. To herself as well, of course, but most of all to her husband.'

He tapped his snuffbox and looked contentedly at the curtain of hail and sleet that ruled out all possibility of moving on. 'First of all, they should never be allowed to learn to read,' he went on, 'it only makes them believe they can think. They confuse what they read in books with the thoughts they don't have for themselves, read a bit here and a bit there, go gadding about the town listening to gossip, hear the odd word being exchanged on a street corner, put two and two together, and before you know it they come up with an opinion to throw in your face. Eugh, an opinion; women shouldn't have opinions! How would it be if women went around thinking things? Where would it all end if they actually happened to be right? No, we must insist on men's rights here: a man can be right, a man can be wrong, but he always stands by his word.'

'Of course,' said Jakob, taking a pinch of snuff from the box Leo held out to him. 'But I do think –'

'Not a bit of it, my boy,' said Leo brusquely, 'you don't

think that at all. Surely it's completely obvious what you think? And anyway, I hadn't finished what I was going to say, I was just coming to the question of marriage. The question of marr-iage,' he repeated, looking pensively up at the icicles hanging from the eaves, 'is quite difficult to understand. Especially when you're young and not alert to what you should be looking for: someone just like yourself, that's what you should be looking for! We're agreed that a woman should restrict herself to the domestic domain and leave the thinking and the opinionating to her husband, but apart from that, similarity is all you need. Look at Wessman for example, ugly as sin, spiteful as the Devil, filthy as a pig and so mean he screams when he shits; how do you think he would have managed if he hadn't dug up a woman exactly like himself? And look at the Mayor and his plump wife, you'll agree they're a happy couple? They share the joys of bed and table, and count their money in between.'

'Hold your tongue,' said Jakob. 'In this town, nobody ever counts anything else; you should know that, you and your damned baize.'

'I forgot,' said Leo plaintively, placing his fat hand on Jakob's arm, 'the boy is in mourning. He's in mourning for his King, prematurely snatched away. And he's not bothered about money, I can see that from the way he runs the business. There's something impressive about people who couldn't care less about money, I've always thought, people with the ability to rise above the sorry circumstances in which the rest of us are forced to live our grey and petty lives.'

'We can go now,' said Jakob. 'It's stopped raining.'

He took Leo by the arm and guided him out to the street. 'Damned unpleasant weather,' muttered Leo as a cart thundered by, sending a wave of dirty water over their shoes.

'Which brings me conveniently to the other side of the matter, the reverse side, which is as gloomy, dismal and depressing as this walk: the ill-matched couple, the imprudent marriage. Do you know anything about that?'

'Not much,' said Jakob. 'Watch out for the puddles.'

'Oh,' said Leo, 'it's so easy to be swept along by your feelings when you're young, so tempting and exciting. Unfortunately, it's part of human nature to think little of yourself and be fascinated only by what's strange and unfamiliar – a fiery temperament if you're sluggish yourself; exuberant good humour if you tend to melancholy; dark colouring if your own face is like a parsnip; all the things that lead you into the dangerous, dark wood where the tree of ill fortune grows, ripping wide the ground with its thick roots and scaring the birds so they screech out loud and fall down dead.'

'It sounds a ghastly place,' Jakob said.

'Ghastly?' cried Leo. 'You can say that again! Sadly, we all too often see examples of alliances like that, where one side has allowed itself to be taken in and the other has indulged in seduction; and it's like mating a pig with a dog: they both feel ashamed of themselves afterwards and there can be no offspring. A beautiful woman who marries an ugly man – what pinpricks she will deal out to the poor wretch! Or if we turn the tables: well, then you can expect not just pinpricks but full-scale torture! Or take a very clever man who marries a stupid woman – how many weeks do you think it will take him to start dreaming of falling chimney stacks and saddle girths coming loose? Economic inequality is a bad thing too, though that's the easiest sort to overcome.' He gave a self-satisfied cough. 'I myself took a wife with a nice little sum, and we've both felt the benefit. Because

I knew how best to handle it, you see, otherwise life would have been hell.'

'How you do talk,' said Jakob, pulling the old man up short as if he were a horse, by tugging at his arm. 'We're here. This is Wessman's house.'

'True,' said Leo gloomily, looking up at the front of a little wooden house with very low windows. 'I suppose I shall go in and talk to my old friend for a while then, however tedious it may be. But first I must just finish off our conversation with the final example, the worst example of all, which really makes the heart ache in the chest of an old man who may be a fool but who has seen his share of the world: the marriage of an intelligent woman to a man who is a touch stupid.

'Of all misfortunes, that is the worst. For her, the misfortune of being able to see everything very clearly, to see the workings of the world as plainly as her own reflection and hear the falsehoods and hypocrisy grating through his talk of what one should and shouldn't do, what one should and shouldn't think. For him, the equally great misfortune of never understanding what she sees, never fathoming the cause of her anxiety, and never being a part of her life except in the contempt she feels for him. Now that is a misfortune whose dimensions I can barely imagine. But I have my suspicions, oh yes, I have my suspicions. And all because he lacked the sense to get himself a wife who was like himself.'

Jakob looked at Leo, at the puffy face with its sagging cheeks, the mean little eyes, the hair plastered forward over the temples, pale and dead as last year's grass. 'But you, of course, were happily married?' he asked slowly.

'Very,' said Leo with a nod. 'Very.'

'Then perhaps you won't mind my asking what she was like, your wife? Since you fitted so well together.'

'Oh,' said Leo and laughed, 'well, it must be obvious to you that she was clever, good-looking, generous, just, and kindness itself, one of God's true angels.' With that he removed his arm from Jakob's grip and limped with surprising speed across the empty street to disappear through Wessman's front door.

CHAPTER 6

It was seven in the evening before they were ready to start. The town hall servant had been to fetch two loaded baskets from the apothecary's shop. The flasks and jars had been unpacked and set out on a long bench; on a table at the other end of the room, the King's naked body had been laid out under a sheet; the windows had been covered with cloth and the doors to the main chamber of the town hall had been locked. 'I hope you are in agreement that we must manage this alone from here on,' said the royal physician to Jakob, who was standing with his back to him mixing dried herbs in a bowl. 'I would have preferred to do this on my own; it was only the extreme shortage of time that obliged me to ask for an assistant. But it will only be us two, for no one else may see him, no one else but I who have seen him so many times before and you, who will not speak to anyone of what you are going to see.'

They were in the room usually used as the aldermen's council chamber. The thick stone walls retained their cellar-like temperature even in summer and now, without a fire, it was so cold that the breath came frosted from their mouths. Jakob opened a flask and poured alcohol over the herbs. I have seen him too, he thought, turning for a moment towards the table, where the outline of a hollowed-out but still wholly human body could be discerned under the stiff linen.

'I shan't speak to anybody,' he said then, and stirred the mixture with a ladle. 'I shan't *want* to speak to anybody.'

'I don't give a damn what your reasons are,' said the physician shortly, 'as long as you do as I say. Pass me the knife and we can make a start.'

His name was Karl Vogel and his face was like a map of the war, a burnt and demolished landscape, purplish from frostbite, in which you could trace the movements of the troops over twenty years. The white, shoulder-length hair was smoothed back, and when he leant over the table, the light rebounded from his gnarled brow and the fleshy tip of his nose which looked as if it had been cloven by a blow, a misjudged blow that had only grazed him. He stood there for a moment, hesitating with his hand held out in mid-air; then he drew aside the sheet with a slow, almost diffident movement. As Jakob cautiously approached, the physician bent his dreadful face over the naked body that was dreadful in another way, yellowish-white and alone.

Jakob saw the man's lips move, but could not catch the words. 'I can't hear,' he shouted, without any idea why he was shouting. He did not want to see the table where the body lay illuminated by wax candles in tall candlesticks, so he concentrated on the great crouching shadow on the wall that was stretching out a hand and gesturing with it. The exhortation was incomprehensible. 'Speak louder,' he said, 'I can't make out what you want.'

'I wasn't talking to you,' said Vogel, straightening up. 'But I did ask you to bring a knife.'

'Yes,' said Jakob, not moving.

'Do it then.'

'But which one? There are so many here.'

'Just bring one that seems good and sharp.'

Jakob went over to the chair on which Vogel had laid out his instruments and made his selection. He saw that the hand he extended towards the knives was trembling and realised the physician would think he was scared, but he was not scared of the dead body, not revolted by its smell, not frightened by the thought of the procedure, the pails standing by the table, the heaps of material torn into rags, not by the cut. He was merely not prepared to see that face close up for the first time and immediately set about destroying it.

'What are you waiting for?' asked Vogel genially. 'Don't you think he's handsome?'

'I don't know,' said Jakob, his finger following the slight curvature of the chosen blade. 'Is he?'

'Come and see.'

Jakob turned and took a few steps towards the table, but Vogel pulled him closer, forced him to face the body and held him fast with a hard grip on his chin. 'Look, then,' he said, 'look at the King. This is what he looks like, this is what he has become. He was not like this before, but this is how he is now; it's not his fault. He wasn't especially handsome even when he was alive.'

'It's not the way he looks that scares me,' said Jakob.

'I know what's scaring you,' said Vogel, releasing his hold. 'You don't like a king who is dead. Only a live one is kingly enough in your eyes, one who sits on a horse and points with his sword so he can be seen from a great distance. But you will have to accept that this one has abdicated for good.'

He leant his hands on the table, and stooped over the naked body for a moment. 'Let me tell you what *I* can see,' he said. 'Here,' he indicated a white scratch on the upper

93

arm, 'here is the memento of an accident with a rapier when he was fourteen. Here on his shoulder something considerably worse, a bullet that time. Luckily it went straight through, as you can see if you turn the body over. Help me then!' he barked, without looking up, and Jakob put his hands under the King's left shoulder and helped to roll him round. 'Here's the exit hole,' said Vogel, pointing to a raised area on the pale skin, 'neat and clean, no complications, all it needed was a firm dressing.'

He went quiet for a moment, muttered to himself as he stroked the little bump on the shoulder with his fingertips and then released his hold so the King rolled back and the arm was hurled out over the edge of the table. Vogel tucked it back in place and quickly moved on to the foot end. 'Here, on the other hand,' he went on, pulling Jacob's head towards him by the collar, 'here we have a really serious problem. You don't believe me? A minor injury to the foot, you say? Let me tell you I nearly lost him that time: an encysted bullet wound that got infected. I had to operate more than once, but because he willed it so badly, the foot healed.'

Jakob looked at the star-shaped indentation in the foot resting in the palm of Vogel's hand, a thin foot, quite small, with long toes and pronounced calluses on the heel. 'Yes, he willed it,' said Vogel, 'it went as he willed. His will was kingly, whatever you think of the rest of him.

'This is the body's language, you see,' he said calmly, straightening up. 'His body talks to me, I understand it. It went without things that others find necessary because it enjoyed doing that – don't be deceived, it didn't suffer. It did what it wanted above all else when it left court and never returned, for it liked sleeping on the ground and washing in cold water. Generally indifferent to most discomforts, resistant to illness, tolerant of pain . . . In short, a body that held out for as long as it could. But a bullet straight into the brain is too much even for a will as kingly as his.'

He crossed his arms, bowed his head and mumbled something to himself. Then he took Jakob by the arm and hustled him to the other end of the table to complete the examination. 'Here,' he said, pointing to the hole in the King's temple, 'see for yourself. There's nothing left, the skull is like a blown egg. And if you don't want to see this broken skull and this body that speaks so plainly and this face that probably bears no resemblance to the pictures you've seen, then I don't want you in here any longer.'

He let go of Jakob's arm and stepped back to the wall. Carefully, so as not to let the wax drip, Jakob took one of the candles from the side table behind them and held it up over the King's head, then he moved it slowly to one side and saw the hole where the bullet had gone in, the sharp edges of bone, the slightly singed hair that was grey at the sides but still dark on the top of the head. The temple had caved in above the ear and there were some pieces of loose bone that looked as if they would come free if you prodded them. When he raised his eyes slightly he could see the King's nose very close to his own, pointed and tinged with blue where the bone was visible under the taut skin. The face had no expression, neither anger nor surprise.

He put back the candle and ran his gaze the length of the body: the feet and the angular kneecaps, the shrivelled sexual organ, the sunken belly and the ribs making folds beneath the loose skin. The arms were thin and wiry and the hands dark brown, just like those of the man he had seen in the square. He held out his own hand and felt the King's rough fingertips and the upturned palm. On the inside of the thumb there was a small scar that Vogel had forgotten, the sort of scar you get when you are whittling and the knife slips.

'That's good,' said Vogel quietly from behind him, 'in fact, it's more than I ask. Now fetch me the straight-bladed knife instead and bring the forceps while you're at it.'

'Well, see, I don't know what I'm supposed to be doing,' said Jakob, standing upright again. 'I mean, I'm no physician.'

'But then nobody has asked you to cure him, have they?' said Vogel. 'I shall tell you if I need help, but this stage is actually no worse than gutting an unusually big fish.'

Jakob took the curved knife and put it back on the chair. When he touched the others they were so cold the metal felt as if it were burning his fingers. He selected the instruments the physician had asked for and laid them on the very edge of the table, while Vogel removed his coat and moved the candles closer to make enough light. 'Pour some aquavit into the silver bowl and then keep out of the way until I need you again,' said the physician curtly; then he took a deep breath and briskly made a long incision in the King's belly.

'Because this is definitely not something you'd enjoy,' he went on after a time. 'I am not enjoying it either, but no one has come up with a better method yet. Of course, they boiled St Birgitta before they transported her home from Rome, but then those papists were happy to make do with the bones. That isn't our way, we want the whole person. Or rather,' he muttered, depositing some of the intestines into the empty pail, 'most of him, at any rate.'

Jakob stood at the other end of the room, holding the bowl and watching him. The moment Vogel took up the knife and set to work, his face changed somehow and became less frightening, which was strange, considering the sort of work it was.

But his face softened and took on a slightly quizzical expression, as if he were wondering about what he saw inside the opened body.

It was a deceptive softness. 'Where did the bullet come from?' asked Jakob on impulse. 'I mean, who fired the shot?'

'How the hell should I know?' said Vogel, reaching for the forceps. 'But maybe the Norwegians are better marksmen than we thought –' He broke off and grunted something as he leant over the body – 'and what's more, shoot their best over long distances. Organs still sound,' was his next comment as he took a brief rest, leaning against the wall, 'amazingly sound in view of the time.' He wiped his hands on a towel and seemed to be doing a mental calculation of the number of days that had passed.

'Don't you want to know?' asked Jakob.

'Of course I do. But I'm not one for fanciful speculation.' He picked up the forceps, bent over the body again and called out: 'Stop talking and bring the bowl over, this is the King's heart.'

Jakob went up to the table where the physician was bending over, rinsing something in a bucket. As he raised the forceps Jakob could see the grey, slightly angular lump of muscle held fast between the two pincers. 'The King's heart,' said Vogel again, rotating it in mid-air, 'a lion's heart in its own way, though that is not visible to ordinary eyes. Looks like any old heart, to be honest, but a royal heart must be treated royally and kept in a silver bowl full of good aquavit. And not only that, the alcohol must be changed every other hour. Don't forget that, and don't dare help yourself to any.'

'No,' said Jakob, and carried the bowl across to the table.

'Now it's time to start the drying,' Vogel went on, 'wipe,

97

wipe, like any cleaning woman. Bring the cloths, and hurry up for God's sake, I'm sick of standing here all wet and messy.'

He held out his hand and snapped his fingers, and Jakob rushed forward with the pieces of cloth and gave them to him one by one. 'There's a fire in the little room,' he said, when he felt the old man's fingers brush against his own, cold as ice.

'Don't get the idea you'll be sitting in there for any length of time,' said Vogel. 'Dry, dry,' he muttered, 'stuff the whole craw full. Then you are to take out this load of shit and burn it. Oh God, the aches and pains in this old body!'

He threw the last of the wet and bloodstained cloths on to the floor and stretched. Suddenly he was grey-faced, old, bent, doddery, as haggard as a tree struck by lightning. 'Never did like cleaning fish,' he said slowly, letting the table take his weight, 'not even when I was a boy. All that shiny stuff slipping through your fingers . . .'

'What must I do?' asked Jakob.

'Wash it all,' said Vogel and gave an abrupt laugh. 'Keep on washing. With alcohol. Every other hour.' He spoke jerkily, in short bursts. 'All night. Wash all night. The King must be immaculately clean.'

'I'm not particularly tired,' said Jakob, 'I can –'

'Most certainly you can,' said Vogel, pushing him aside. 'But now I shall go out and have a good scrub. Warm myself for a while, smoke a pipe and take a nip. Meanwhile, you can familiarise yourself more closely with a human's inside, which is not particularly exciting when it is empty and actually quite similar to a lion's. Or a pig's for that matter, since I assume you have more experience of pigs than lions. Saw one in Germany,' he mumbled. 'Stuffed of course, but even so. One imagines,' he called, on the point of shutting the door, 'that their hearts are so much bigger. I don't know why. Maybe because they run so fast.'

Left alone, Jakob kicked the rags into a corner beside the covered pail and moved the candles back to make a softer light round the table. He poured alcohol into a bowl and washed the body, first the inside which was clean and virtually dry, then the outside, which was covered in abraded grey skin that came off on the sponge. He used a different sponge for the face, wiping it very carefully over the eyelids and lips where the skin was at its thinnest, then applying firmer pressure across the cheeks, up to the forehead and the receding hairline. When Vogel came back, they helped each other turn the body and wash the back; then they both went out together to the little room where the town hall manservant was keeping the fire stoked and there was food and aquavit laid out on the table between the two armchairs. 'No,' said Vogel as they sat down. 'We will have every need of the drink but I fear the food will go to waste. I defy anybody to sit down to a plate of ham on such an evening.'

He had regained his composure and was as calm as at their initial meeting, though more kindly disposed to Jakob, who sat slumped in his armchair, drugged by the warmth that was making his fingers redden and swell. Vogel smoked his pipe and told Jakob a little about what he wanted him to do during the night, and about various compounds he had devised for the ointment they would apply to the body once the washing process was complete. Jakob listened, drank, stirred up the fire, stretched out his numbed feet towards it and wiggled his toes in the warmth. When Vogel had fallen asleep, he went over to the window that gave on to the inner courtyard and looked at the starry sky; it had grown colder once more, which meant that the wet snow churned up by many wheels would freeze into jagged formations and make the roads passable only with great difficulty. No people were to be seen and no sound penetrated the thick walls which shut him in with a sleeping man and a dead one. Then Vogel awoke and they went back into the little council chamber and washed the body again.

The candles burnt down and were replaced with new ones; the cask of aquavit standing alongside the physician's pestles and mortars was emptied by the many washings, the repeated, monotonous strokes of the sponge over the body that tolerated everything and allowed itself to be opened and lifted by the two men who had virtually stopped talking. Between washings Vogel slept, but Jakob could not sleep; he sat wide awake in his chair as the sky paled, he stood at the window in the grey dawn light and saw a cart clatter in through the gate with the new coffin of polished oak, saw it unloaded and carried in. He did the last washing alone, for now he had learnt all the manoeuvres and needed no help to lift and turn the light, white body. He strained the herbs out of the alcohol solution and bathed the body with the extract, which had a slight scent of mint and hay.

Then he took off his shirt and had a wash in the hot water the servant had brought in. Vogel was still asleep, in a streak of sunlight that moved across his slack face; he batted at it without waking up. The time was getting on for eleven o'clock. Jakob poured himself some coffee and drank it at the window, looking out at the blindingly white rectangle between the walls of the building; he was just thinking that he would go out for a breath of air when the gate in the fence opened and two people crept in, clinging to one another, stiff in their black clothes and with heads bowed as if they were obliged to keep their eyes fixed on the ground to avoid falling over.

They looked so small and lost out in the big courtyard that he failed to recognise them until the man took off his hat and called something to him and the woman looked up, shading her eyes with her hand against the bright sunlight. Then he called out 'I'm coming', although he knew they could not hear, grabbed his coat and hurried down the stairs and out into the morning air that was so cold it made his teeth ache. For a brief moment, he was simply happy at being whole and alive and able to feel the contrast between the warmth up there in the room and the biting cold here outside; then he saw their frightened faces and felt frightened himself. They were holding on to each other and Sofie was looking at Mattias all the time, but he was looking at the wall as if unaware of her standing beside him, hugging his arm. 'Has anything happened?' Jakob asked, but Sofie shook her head and said: 'All is well with us.'

'No,' Mattias said slowly, 'nothing has happened. I've just been for a little talk with the Dean and now I'm going to talk to Karl Vogel and then we shall go home for dinner. And then . . .'

'Then you really must have a little rest,' said Sofie, but Mattias furrowed his brow and muttered something about a carriage still not being ready.

'What carriage is that?' asked Jakob, and Mattias told him in great detail, and as slowly as if he were only half awake, that it was a specially made carriage, so the coffin could be transported up to Stockholm without getting damaged on the bad roads, as if in a cradle. 'Absolutely ingenious,' he mumbled, 'no expense spared, let's just hope it's ready in time.'

'It will be,' said Sofie.

'And the church service will be tomorrow evening,' went on Mattias, 'as soon as you and Vogel have finished here. Then they'll be off, you know, riding away in their specially commissioned carriage with its specially devised suspension, but we will have to stay here and deal with all the rest, we'll be quite alone. But not for long, no, for there will soon be more coming.'

He suddenly put his arm round Jakob's shoulders and pulled him to him so all three of them were standing close together, and said gravely: 'If I have said anything to you these last days that has hurt you, I hope you can forgive me for it.'

'You haven't said anything,' said Jakob. 'I'm not hurt.'

'Oh?' said Mattias. 'I thought perhaps . . . but it's all the same. Yes,' he said, straightening up, 'it really is all the same. In times like these one can't afford to be too sensitive. Now I shall exchange a few words with the physician and then we'll go home and eat. You talk to Sofie in the meantime and try to make her understand . . . Just try to make her understand, because I can't.' He jammed his hat down on to his head, freed himself from their embrace and went quickly over to the back door of the town hall.

Jakob watched the stocky little figure go, holding itself erect and kicking out at the lumps of ice lying in its path so they shattered like glass against the solid stone walls. 'What's the matter with him?' he asked. 'It felt just as if he was saying farewell.'

'He's saying farewell to everything,' said Sofie sadly. 'He believes the world is going under. But if it does, he will be the last person to save himself and reach dry land, of course.'

'Are you going to say farewell to me, too?' asked Jakob.

'No, but I don't think we shall be seeing each other as often from now on. I don't know why, I just have a feeling. That everything is going to be different now.'

How do you mean, different? he would have like to ask her, but she suddenly went quiet and leant against the wall. 'Isn't the sun beautiful?' she whispered. 'Isn't the light wonderful? How can he think I'd be willing to go and sit in a church and cry over someone I've never met? It's immoral, full mourning like that with black drapery and drummers and strangers in the front pews and the Dean polishing and polishing his sermon and unable to talk to his wife because he has to spare his voice. It's quite, quite ludicrous! Soon I shall think everything's ludicrous.'

'Surely not Mattias?'

'No,' she said gently, 'not Mattias. Because he thinks it's ludicrous too. If we were to discuss it, we'd laugh ourselves to death! The carriage-maker who's beside himself with delight although he hasn't been paid an öre, and the Dean with his scarf wound round half his face and his poor wife running up and down with her honey drinks . . . It's as Mattias says, soon we will be left alone here and they will scarcely remember the name of this town once they have ridden away. How will things turn out for us?'

'Well,' he said, 'it will all turn out well.'

She put her arm through his and they took a few turns about the courtyard while she spoke of her children, as she often did when they were alone; of the boy who was so headstrong and difficult and the girl who was so stubborn and intelligent. She said they were both so spoilt that they always assumed people meant them well; and if they heard a raised voice it did not even alarm them, because they could not conceive of the possibility that someone might be cross with them and telling them off. 'They think it's just a game,' she said. 'If I ever shout, they act as if I were out of my senses; they feel a little uncomfortable on my behalf but not in the least afraid.'

'But you mustn't think any less of the others,' she said quickly, setting down her basket on the ground so she had both arms free to show him how large her family of children was, and how richly endowed with little, individual features that differentiated them although they were basically all alike, and all equally loved. 'The youngest boy was so calm and his sister always made me laugh. And their big brother was really the most beautiful of them all, very like his father . . . But of course, they are all beautiful.'

'Of course.'

'Yet there was something special about him, even so. People could never stop looking at him, they had never seen such lovely blue eyes before or such delicate hands, like in a painting. Though the others were never jealous.'

'Goes without saying!'

'Hardly ever quarrelled . . . Strange, siblings usually do quarrel . . . But my children aren't like others.'

'You could always take them out into the country, you know,' said Jakob, 'if you're worried.'

'I was thinking about it. Perhaps we will go to the country after Christmas.'

He took her hand, turned it over in his own and studied it. He liked her hands because they were as small as toys, yet work-hardened nonetheless. As always when he was alone with Sofie, he felt a mild and slightly melancholy longing to confide in her, tell her something he had never told anybody else. He had no idea what, nor did it matter, because all he really wanted was to yield and soften, stammer something incoherent and perhaps moan a little about the thing he scarcely recalled, complaining because he did not want to remember or because he could not. His blue sorrow had no name. It was like the evenings when the blackbird sang and the song sounded like a forgotten path through the forest that you might be able to find again if only you kept looking long enough.

She had always stopped him and thus saved them both from that moment of mute embarrassment afterwards. But this time she might have let him speak, she might have listened; and if Mattias had not come back out into the courtyard at that moment and called her, she might even have answered and said that there was no true sorrow but death, the sorrow of bereavement. But Mattias interrupted them, and at once she pulled away, picked up her basket and ran off.

Jakob watched them go as they disappeared through the open gate, feeling nothing more than a superficial envy of the strong grasp that united the two bodies. They were as alike as brother and sister, as two silver spoons in a case, as two loaves put to rise on the same baking sheet, golden yellow and wholesome. Like eating yourself, he thought, sleeping with yourself, talking to yourself. Just loving yourself, that can't be hard. It was as well he had not had time to utter those words which after all would not have been the same colour as his feelings.

He did not miss them, for as soon as he entered the town hall Vogel, now fully awake, was telling him about things that needed preparing. In the course of the day he occasionally felt a sort of aching sensation, tried to work out what it was and then remembered: they had made their farewells. But then he forgot it again, until the dull ache

105

roused him some hours later and he was obliged to scour his memory until he found the cause: Oh yes, of course, he thought again, it's because they said farewell.

While Vogel washed the body cavities with herbal extract, he began preparing the ointment and strangely enough found himself taking pleasure in handling the jars with Tobias's carefully written labels, measuring out aloe, cumin, violet root and myrrh, weighing things out on the scales and grinding things in the big mortar, melting wax and tallow in a pot over the fire and mixing it all to an aromatic paste. He enjoyed stirring it to make it smooth and watching it cool and thicken, but Vogel was in a bad mood and swearing at the body, perhaps because his own was paining him so severely in the cold. The wind had got up outside and they were wading in the floor-level draught as if in icy water. 'Bodies,' muttered Vogel, 'dead or alive, they're nothing but trouble.' Then he slapped the King as if he were a side of bacon and limped back out to the warmth.

'Have you ever been up in the mountains?' Jakob asked, once they had sat down and pulled up their chairs. He poured some wine for the physician, who took the cup in both hands like a child.

'I've been in Russia,' said Vogel, 'isn't that enough? These damned mountains everyone's always going on about.'

'I only want to know –'

'I *know* what you want to know, I always do. There's no better way to get to know a person than to watch his expression as he turns over a dead body. But all I know about the troops is that they were spread along the border when I left them; it is quite likely some battalions tried to take a short cut over the mountains to the Swedish side, and if they found someone to show them the way it'll be all right. Reliable guides, quiet weather, warm clothes and plenty of fuel and they'll be fine.

'Naturally one can imagine the Norwegians not being at all eager to go ahead and show them the way,' he went on, holding out his wine cup for a refill, 'but you can always get round that with a generous tip or a rope round the waist or a pistol to the head. Of course, it may be blowing as much of a gale up there as it is here; it'll be colder, at any rate. And they aren't likely to find much to make a fire with, or clothes . . . Hmm, you might well think that a king who has trudged through the snows of the Ukraine should have the sense to supply his men with proper gloves? But what do I know, after all I'm not there, I'm here and drinking myself warm and keeping myself busy with the lad in there. And I'm bloody glad of it; gets me out of sawing and that's the worst thing I know: sawing, sawing, barrel loads of hands and feet no one needs any more. Good Lord, yes, it's going to be an excellent year for hunting up in the mountains. Fat animals with glossy coats, that will be the Norwegians' compensation.'

He took out his pipe and fumbled to fill it, lit it with a glowing splint of wood and disappeared with a sigh into a cloud of smoke. It was already dark outside, but they did not bother to ask for candles, making do with the firelight. The soot is burning, thought Jakob, that means there'll be a storm. He listened to the wind, which was getting up and growling at the gaps round the windows; then he cut himself a piece of smoked sausage and wolfed it down, his hand over his mouth to conceal his unseemly hunger. 'Though animals take no account of borders,' said Vogel thoughtfully, 'so the Swedes will be getting some first-rate skins as well.

'No,' he went on, 'I've never been up on the mountains,

107

but I know how people look when they freeze to death. They swell up and go all grey in the face and then they lie down. Or sit down, I've seen them sitting in a circle round a fire long gone out, snowed over so only their hats were sticking out, like tree stumps. Some were sitting dead in their sleighs with the reins in their hands, others on horseback, coated in ice. I've even seen them standing dead in the snow, as stiff and rigid as corn poles. They say the cold lets you die a beautiful death, but that's not how it looked. These were pulling terrible faces behind the ice.'

Jakob tried to visualise a mountainside open to the elements, treeless and with a single trampled track being obliterated by the wind. But the warmth was too intense, and beside him Vogel happened to let his cup slip, spilling wine down the front of his shirt; he shot up out of his chair with an oath and roared: 'Törn, be so good as to go out to the treatment room and coat the body cavities with tincture!' And Jakob forgot the mountains for the body on the table, the wax candles that had almost burnt down, the window coverings that were flapping in the draught and needed rehanging. He sponged the inside of the chest and the abdominal cavity with the pungent alcohol and then sprinkled on a handful of crushed herbs. He could hear the physician moving around in the next room, bellowing for candles and wine, thumping on a door and then sinking back into his chair, which creaked beneath his weight.

When Jakob went back out to him he had put one leg up on a stool and taken out a little black notebook which he was consulting. 'Twenty-four hours,' he mumbled, turning the pages with his fat fingers, 'that means we can start the final phase about midday tomorrow. We mustn't disrupt the Mayor's timetable.' He licked his finger, turned to another page and intoned in a hollow voice: 'Rose oil, oil of spike lavender, turpentine and resin,' then fell silent and his purple face drooped in heavy folds over his shirt collar.

He seemed deeply unhappy. As the wind hurled itself against the window with a howl, shaking the glass and dislodging a shower of soot and old mortar that went rattling down the chimney pipe, he gave a start, dropped his notebook and said sharply: 'But you, Jakob Törn, living here on the margins of the kingdom with your wife and your inherited business – which to judge by your dexterity you doubtless run extremely well – you think, I suppose, that we are born into this world to make the best of our life? Is that what you think, eh?'

'Perhaps I do,' said Jakob, since that seemed to be the answer expected of him.

'But I don't,' said Vogel. 'I think we are born to waste our life, squander it on things that lead nowhere, ruin it so we accustom ourselves to setting no store by it. The point is to make us stop believing it's worthwhile.'

'At least there's a point then.'

'Too damned right there's a point, that's what I'm telling you! The point of life is for us to ruin it.'

'But a point . . . assumes there's someone who invents that point,' said Jakob slowly. 'And it's not definite that God exists, is it?'

'Of course He exists,' roared Vogel. 'Surely it's perfectly obvious He exists, even if He has some slightly strange ideas. God exists for us not to be able to believe in Him, don't you see? The wind exists for us not to be able to catch it, the sun exists to make us realise how cold we are, standing in the shade. It's all infernally well devised to teach us what real life is, namely the abandonment of even the most modest expectations. We may begin with an extravagant amount of capital, but He will take it from us in the end, even so. He plans well ahead, He has time on His side, God. In the end He always gets His way.'

'I don't care about God,' said Jakob, 'but most of the people I know would describe Him very differently.'

'I can well believe it,' said Vogel fervently. 'They're still clinging on for all they are worth; you can beat a dog for years before it bites back. Most people in this world are more than ready to let themselves be abused. I don't suppose for a moment they enjoy the pain, but perhaps in their imagination they can see their reward, a reward that will make up for all the thrashings they've taken. Poor devils.'

'And what's the difference between them and you?' Jakob asked.

'None. None at all, except that I have a clearer view of God's wonderful design, which is not to heal but to sever, not to open but to close. Knock at the gates, and you will as sure as damn it find them bolted and barred. He wants us broken, because that's the only way He likes us, as limp and floppy as rag dolls.

'And now we're supposed to go around being heartbroken with grief into the bargain,' he went on, screwing up his face in the pretence that it was contorted with tears. 'Boo-hoo, and of course it's because they have lost their good shepherd that the men are falling off their horses, not because the wind is so strong it can tear them from their saddles and hurl the horses to their knees. No, we're little lambs lost in the snow, with no good shepherd to lead us home again. Boo-hoo-hoo. So what shall we do? Get ourselves a new one as soon as we've finished crying?'

'I don't know,' said Jakob.

'No, who the hell does? I expect no pronouncements from you, you're only here to listen. Now go and repeat the procedure with the sponge, because I intend getting some sleep.'

But he did not go to sleep, and when Jakob returned he was sitting stooped over, resting his chin in one hand and massaging his foot with the other. He was staring into the fire, which had been transformed into a palace of embers with tall spires that crumbled and immediately rose again in new formations. Jakob threw on a couple of logs and snatched a slice of bread from the tin plate on the table. 'You eat by all means,' said Vogel amiably. 'It doesn't bother me.'

'I suppose you'll be going home now the war's over?' asked Jakob, turning to him.

'Ah, I shouldn't be so sure of that. If you haven't been home for twenty years it's not just a matter of kicking off your boots and marching straight in, you have to get used to the idea first. Twenty years,' he muttered, 'that sounds bad, it sounds like half a lifetime. It didn't feel long, it felt like nothing. And yet it's quite long enough for a person to be born, grow up, develop into adulthood, get ideas, learn to contradict. I have one son buried in Poland and one who's a prisoner of war in Tobolsk, but I also have a son back at home who's twenty and has never seen his father. Perhaps he exists for me never to be able to see him? The war could start all over again, like it has so many times before.'

Jakob nodded and leant his head against the backrest. He thought Vogel was still talking and heard himself reply, but in actual fact he was fast asleep and only awoke two hours later, when the town hall manservant came in, yawning, with a new jug of hot water for Vogel, who was standing washing in the corner with a towel slung over his shoulder. They shared a salt herring and drank a toast to the King who had wasted his own and others' lives to no purpose at all and borne out the physician's philosophy.

To Jakob, this second night seemed to go more quickly than the first. Now it was his turn to sleep and the physician's turn to stay awake, bent over the pillowcase he was holding between his knees to fill with rose petals, southernwood, sweet woodruff, mint and St John's wort. 'For sweet dreams,' he explained, 'and the scent of the hay meadow.' As day dawned they took a few turns about the courtyard, then Vogel stretched out on the sofa and pulled his coat over his face while Jakob took charge of the final applications of tincture.

It seemed to him the body had changed in some perplexing way. Or perhaps he was the one who had changed, since he now found it beautiful to behold, white and bewitching, smelling of alcohol and flowers, as simple as a smoothly ground stone or a piece of wood. He wiped the sponge over it and arranged the arms in such a way that the incision was hidden, though not even that disturbed him much now. It was merely an opening that could be closed.

He had just unpacked a bundle of linen and started tearing it into swaddling strips when Vogel opened the door and came in. Without a word the physician went slowly across to the table, picked up a candlestick from the side table and held it above the King's transformed face, which by this time was so unlike his own grey, exhausted one. 'I had a dream,' he whispered, reaching out to touch the thin hair, the peaceful hands folded on the breast. 'It was such a strange dream it must be true. I dreamt he was talking to me.'

He turned round and looked about him with the candle held aloft. 'It was this room,' he went on, 'this table, the body was lying exactly as it is now. Everything was exactly

112

as it is now. I was just going to turn it over and sponge the back when the King opened his eyes and said my name. "Vogel," he said. Twice he said my name and I answered as I always do: "Yes, Your Majesty!" Then he took hold of both my hands and said, "You must bear witness to how I was shot." His fingers were like ice and I whispered, "Your Majesty, please be so gracious as to tell me whether the shot came from the fort." Then he raised his right hand, moved it back and forth three times in front of my face and said, "No, Vogel. Someone crept up."'

Jakob put the bundle of linen down on the bench. 'Someone crept up,' he said, and looked at the physician, who was stooping over with the candle so close to the King's head that a few of the brown hairs hissed and frizzled. 'Vogel, what does that mean?'

'Someone who knew where to look,' whispered the physician, 'someone who knew where to aim. Someone crept up, an insider, from home, close enough to be sure of not missing, someone came crawling on hands and knees through the snow . . .'

'It could have happened like that.'

'I know, I know,' said Vogel. 'But now he's saying it really did, and whom should I tell, apart from you? Who would believe me?' He set the candle back down on the side table, clasped his hands behind his back and shambled out into the anteroom without closing the door behind him, so Jakob could then see him sitting by the fire, bent and melancholy, with the pipe he had forgotten to light.

Outside it was day now, with a leaden light from the thick mass of cloud and a hard wind sweeping the new snow across the courtyard. Jakob tried to persuade the physician to drink a little coffee, but he clenched his teeth round his cold pipe and pushed the bread plate disdainfully away. They heard voices outside, urgent footsteps on the stairs and a clattering as the coffin was heaved up and set down outside the door, but they took no notice, concentrating instead on preventing flakes of ash from whirling up and getting into the pan of wax that was slowly melting over the fire.

Around midday they began the final phase. Jakob's job was to stand beside Vogel and hold out the bowl while the physician carefully coated the body cavities with ointment, which had set to the consistency of honey. He grunted as he worked, sighed as he got to the more inaccessible parts and tried to let some light fall into the dark recesses to see that all the surfaces were covered and ready.

Then the silver bowl was brought, the heart was lifted out of its alcohol bath, dried with a napkin, coated in oils and put back into the breast. Without a word about lions, courage or stamina, Vogel with his assurance and dexterity resembled nothing so much as a mason putting the last stone in place. He thrust his hands into the bowl of spices, smelt them for a moment and then filled the cavities until the body was rounded and filled out. This done, he straightened up, took the needle with its thick, resin-coated thread, held it up in front of Jakob's eyes and said: 'Will you sew up His Majesty's stomach or shall I?'

Jakob did not reply. He went over and leant against the wall, listening to the wind whistling in the chimneys and the curious sound of thread being pulled through skin. It felt as if he had never been anywhere else but in this cold room with all the candles and the great shadow sweeping its right arm across the wall in even, regular movements. 'Alcohol,' called the physician, and he opened the bottle and stood alongside to watch as the sewed-up body was washed for the last time. 'Ointment,' called the physician, and he brought the bowl and helped to turn and roll the body and anoint it from the brow to the soles of the feet. Then he dipped the strips of fabric in a mixture of wax and oil and handed them one by one to Vogel, who wound them round the body with handfuls of herbs between the layers. The body disappeared inside a swaddling of stiff bandage with a scent of the linen cupboard. 'Uniform,' called the physician, and Jakob brought the clean coat and trousers that had been lying folded on a chair by the door and helped to put them on the body, which was now stiff, unyielding and hard to deal with. Vogel adjusted the stockings, polished the toecaps of the shoes with his sleeve, did up the last button and gave the collar a quick tug to hide the linen beneath. 'They can take him now,' he said with satisfaction. 'He looks smart now. He looks like a king now.'

They went out on to the staircase to fetch the coffin. In the big mirror that hung outside the Mayor's office, Jakob saw the image of two hollow-eyed men laughing out loud as the coffin slipped from their grasp, hit the floor and lost its lid; two unshaven men blinking in the light and starting like nervous animals at the sound of someone moving in the adjoining room. Once they had manhandled the coffin into the council chamber and laid out the body on the white silk, Vogel went to get the pillow he had prepared and inserted it under the King's head; then he took a little leather bag from his breast pocket and placed it by the King's right foot. 'The bit of bone,' he explained, 'the one I took out when I operated.' Suddenly Jakob noticed he was crying, real tears this time, running down his nose and dripping on to the shining face on the pillow. They fitted the lid in place and Jakob went out to the stairs to call the men in.

They stood by the window as the coffin was carried out. They could see the hearse down in the courtyard, the horses with their black plumes, the crowd parting to let the bearers through and then forming up behind the carriage as it set off with a jolt and moved out into the street. The mourners struggled after it in the strong wind that blew their torches into white balls of fire. 'You could have gone with them,' said Jakob, but the physician shook his head and went to the council chamber to collect up his instruments.

'So could you,' he said after a while, passing Jakob two empty glass jars. Jakob put them in the basket from the shop and went on washing bowls in a pail of warm, soapy water. They worked slowly and sleepily side by side, quiet and alone in the big, dark house in the little, dark town whose inhabitants had left their homes to gather at the church. The doors were to be left open to let everybody hear the hymn singing and see the coffin. But nobody would be allowed to see the King.

Once Vogel had stowed away the last of the things in his chest and shut the lid, he put out all the candles round the table, went into the little anteroom and sat down in his chair. 'I shall spend the night here,' he said, pouring the last of the wine into his cup. Jakob looked about the room, saw the firewood was all gone and put the physician's coat to hand on the empty chair. Without turning his head Vogel said: 'You'll be off home now, I suppose?'

'Yes,' said Jakob.

'Good,' said the physician. With a deep sigh he covered himself with his coat, put one foot on the stool and leant his head back. He seemed to be asleep, but Jakob knew that he was wide awake, would stay awake all night and be ready the next morning to continue the next stage of the journey.

He took his rest like a horse, one leg at a time, heedless of the darkness and the cold that came creeping along the floor.

'You do have a home, I suppose?' mumbled Vogel. 'Everyone has a home. Go home now, Jakob Törn, and celebrate Christmas Eve.'

Neither of them said goodbye. They had been shut in together for two days and nights. Only two days and nights, thought Jakob as he stopped on the town hall steps and filled his lungs with ice-cold air.

Four days and nights had passed since he had crashed to the floor in Sofie's drawing room and disrupted the card game, three days and nights since he had hidden behind some barrels outside his own house while a candle was lit in the window, three weeks since he had got up from his bed one night and seen a courier racing past with bad news in his knapsack. He had told her about it and she had picked up the knife from the dinner table and plunged it into his arm. He did a calculation and found that the physician was right: it really was Christmas Eve. Now he could go in any direction he pleased, south to the Mayor's house, north to his own, straight along the river to the warehouse or even further afield. He was free, but he did not feel free, and then he suddenly remembered: it was because there was someone waiting for him.

At that he broke into a run; he put his head down and ran. Coat flapping like a sail, he fell down the steps; he thought he was running but instead he fell headlong into a snowdrift and realised something had happened to his leg. Still running, he swore at the leg and pummelled at it with his fists, but then he got to his feet and almost immediately found his way back into his old gait, the old swaying, rolling motion that must look so ridiculous. It didn't matter. He extended his arms and used his hands for propulsion, finding support in the air and laughing at himself.

It had started snowing again, a dense fall of hard little snowflakes. He did not want to stop to do up his coat, he had already lost so much time. After a while he found he was making speedy progress, now he had found the rhythm. Two streets from home he was obliged to lean against a wall and catch his breath for a moment, and that was when he saw the first soldiers looming up out of the dark.

CHAPTER 7

When Jakob opened the front gate of his home, he saw the courtyard was covered in footprints and the kitchen door had been left wide open. He rushed up the stairs, where the rust-coloured marks from that last morning still stained the walls, paused for a moment outside the door to the living quarters and then climbed the rest of the way to the attic on the rickety stepladder he had never got round to replacing. He went straight into Lars Björnson's room without knocking, but it was empty; the writing desk had been cleared and the bedclothes removed. He went over to the window and looked down into the courtyard where the light from the door was falling on the blood-spattered rotunda where the pig had danced and kicked its last and on Maret, who was standing in the middle with her apron over her head.

Fatigue suddenly hit him. He gripped the window sill, propping his forehead against the glass for a moment, then climbed slowly back down through the deathly silent house and went out into the courtyard where the girl was weeping, the pail she had filled and brought out from sheer habit thrown down beside her in the snow. 'You'll have a new pig in the spring, you know,' he said, and took hold of the back of her bodice as one might take a puppy by the scruff of the neck, lifting her in front of him into the warmth. 'I'd rather have a cat,' she said in a muffled voice from inside the layer of fabric. 'Because you'd let it live past Christmas and I could have it in bed with me, too.'

'A pig *and* a cat, then,' he said wearily, drawing up a chair to the fire. His wet shirt had started feeling chilly to his back and he huddled up to the fire as she blew her nose behind him and poured water into a kettle. 'Give me a little,' he asked, and she passed over the water scoop. 'Something to eat, too,' he added, and she went snivelling to the larder to fetch a loaf and some dripping.

'You mustn't go on like that every single year,' he said, once he had taken his first bite. 'You're glad enough of the pork, after all.'

'It's not just the pig, it's everything,' she said, sitting down beside him and putting her feet on the hearth. 'Nobody talks to me, Elisa's up tramping about all night and the notary is ill. And you're not even here, are you? It's all so boring.'

'Why is Lars Björnson's room empty?' Jakob asked.

'We put him in the bedroom instead, where he'd be a bit warmer. And now it's Christmas Eve and I've got to sit here on my own when what I wanted was to go to church and look at the King. I took him some honey in hot water, but he didn't want it.'

'What about Tobias, where's he?'

'Don't know,' she said grumpily. 'Elisa said she was going to fetch the doctor, but that was hours ago. I'd boiled up the bones and made some cabbage soup and after that she went outside and threw up; and then it's to and fro all night, right outside the window so I can never get any sleep. It's like a haunted house. I don't want to be here any more.' She rubbed her face with her dirty sleeve, looked up at him and said: 'Did you really mean what you said about the cat?'

The kettle had begun to sing softly, but otherwise everything was quiet; there were no footsteps from upstairs and the sounds from the street did not penetrate the thick walls. Jakob moved closer to the fire and took another bite of his bread and dripping, for now he was home he could no longer imagine why he had been in such a rush. Lars is alive, he thought. Maret produced some knitting, a half-finished stocking, from her apron pocket and began counting stitches, and with his chin resting on his chest Jakob slept for a few seconds before an exploding spark shot out of the fire and woke him.

'*Where* does she go tramping?' he asked, suddenly wide awake, staring at Maret who was pursuing the spark with skirts held high and clogs stamping.

'Out in the snow, like I said. She goes to and fro outside the window, sighing.'

'You must have dreamt it,' he said, and got to his feet. 'I'm going upstairs now, and when Tobias comes, tell him I want to speak to him. And I want something proper to eat, as well.'

'But he won't come,' she said, 'I know it. He looked so important when he went off, like one of them ministers. Everybody's got so many secrets.' She went up to him and whispered: 'I heard the King rose up out of his coffin and pointed at the person who shot him.'

'That's just a made-up story,' said Jakob. 'The King's dead, he can't do any pointing. Dish out some of the soup and bring it up to me in the dining room.'

'Well, that's what I heard, anyway,' she said sulkily, 'from someone going past in the street, and they said he sat up and pointed and everybody fell down on the floor in a faint because his face looked so gruesome, all bloody with a huge bandage. And the guilty man died on the spot so they didn't have to bother killing him. Of terror.'

'Rubbish,' said Jakob and pushed her aside, making her ball of wool fall on the floor and roll under a table. In the hallway he paused for a moment and opened the door to the courtyard, but there was no one out there and the doors of all the outbuildings were shut, so he went on up to the dining room and set his candle down on the table, where the dishes had been left from dinner with their cold cabbage and rings of congealing white fat.

A half-eaten apple sat shrivelling on the mantelpiece and a shawl hung from the back of a chair as if it had snagged and got caught there when somebody ran past. He folded it up and held it in his arms for a moment, then knocked on the door leading to the bedroom and went in without waiting for an answer, into the close little room where Lars lay propped up in the bed with all the pillows behind his back, looking at him. 'Are you alone?' he asked, and Jakob nodded, looking about him at the roughly drawn curtains, the washbowl with just enough water to cover the bottom, set on a chair beside the bed, and the green carafe glinting on the table beside an empty glass. The doors of the tiled stove were open but the fire was almost out, and he tossed in the last of the wood and blew furiously. 'Good,' said Lars, 'you blow, I'm freezing. Blow for all you're worth.' As the fire caught and it grew lighter, Jakob saw that his lips were blue.

He brought the candle from the dining room and put it on the bedside table, sent the empty wood basket crashing down the stairs, shouted for hot water, spread a blanket over the foot end of the bed, put the shawl round Lars's shoulders and finally went to work with the poker on the inner

122

window until the wooden frame splintered so he could take it out and open the outer window to the night air, which came rushing into the room with its sharp smell of snow. He emptied the washbowl out of the window and rinsed it out with some of the water Maret brought up, pushed the chair aside with his foot and with a single heave moved the bed closer to the fire, which was burning brightly in the cross-draught. From the corner cupboard on the wall of the dining room he brought a jar and a bottle, measured out some powder into a glass, filled it from the carafe and poured warm water into the bowl along with a few drops of oil. 'Mint,' said Lars, and sighed as the strong scent spread through the room. Jakob dipped a piece of cloth into the water and wiped Lars's face, which was cold and sticky with sweat.

'There aren't many smells I can stand,' said Lars, closing his eyes. 'Pork and cabbage aren't among them, but mint is all right. Air, snow, smoke and burning wood, anything light enough to blow about. Perhaps it's because I'm in the midst of a transformation myself that I prefer transient things to fixed ones.'

'You're not going to die yet,' said Jakob, stirring the contents of the glass, 'not yet awhile.' He put his arm round Lars's shoulders, sat him up and said: 'Drink this.'

'I don't see how I could possibly be cured by anything that tastes this bitter,' said Lars once he had swallowed the cloudy liquid.

'You won't be cured,' said Jakob, 'you'll just be able to sleep a bit better.' He carefully loosened the band that fastened Lars's hair at the nape of his neck, drew his fingers through it to get the worst tangles out and lowered his head on to the pillow again.

Then he moved the candle closer to the bed, pulled up a

chair and sat down. Now, while Lars had his eyes shut, he could look at him. He knew Lars was young, younger than himself, but age had disappeared along with everything else and now he was simply who he was, a man who at times looked like a very old child, at times a young woman. And at times like something else that was not a human at all but an object. He leant forward and gently prodded the hand that was lying like a picture of a hand on the sheet, but it felt warm and was withdrawn with a jerk. Lars opened his eyes and said: 'If it can't cure me, let's not bother with the medicine.'

He sounded aggrieved, as if someone had tried to get rid of him. 'It's good for you to get some sleep,' Jakob said.

'Artificially induced sleep is only for healthy people, and for my part I'd rather be awake. Not to think, but to listen. I should like to lie here a while longer and listen; I've always been bad at listening, I've never tried hard enough. At the moment, for example, I can hear Maret singing, down in the kitchen.'

'That's impossible,' said Jakob and smiled.

'She's singing of a knight, and she's the maiden sitting beneath the linden tree combing her hair of spun gold, with a little hind on her lap. In a little while, you'll go down and say you're sorry for shouting at her.'

'What else can you hear?'

'The candle on the bedside table. Its voice is tiny, like a mosquito's, but sometimes it hisses. There's a cracked window pane somewhere and the wind is whistling through it. And the clock in the dining room that I never used to notice, now I can hear every tick.'

'Is it disturbing you?'

'Not at all. Do you ever listen to the fire? I've done it all too rarely. This one has just eaten a lump of fir resin and is spitting out the bits. It sounds as though the fire has rather thick lips tonight. The best sound is the vast one we have around us all the time; and I don't mean the noises from down in the town, but the one that starts when there is no sound, a sort of murmur. Is it people's breathing? Or is it the sound of their thoughts? The thoughts of a mass of people living packed together – why shouldn't we be able to hear them? Perhaps I shall be able to see them soon, as well. Rather like cirrus clouds but nearer the ground.'

'I want you to take this,' said Jakob, pouring out drops into a spoon. 'It will help your heart.'

'You don't understand,' said Lars, 'I've done everything all too rarely!' He turned his head to the window and the muffled sound of feet staggering and shuffling through the snow. 'There must be thousands of them,' he whispered.

'Yes,' said Jakob. He crossed to the window and looked down for a moment on the grey men before pulling the window closed and latching it.

'No one actually knows what it is that destroys some people sooner than others,' said Lars in a shrill voice. 'I don't know anything about hearts, but I know I feel fine. Why shouldn't I, lying here in the warm? I've nothing to complain about, have I? I feel fine, I tell you, and if only I didn't have to breathe I'd be completely content, because it feels as though there's something lying on my chest. And though it isn't heavy in itself, I don't like having it there!'

'There's nothing on your chest,' said Jakob. 'Only the quilt.'

'I know it's only the quilt, do you think I'm an idiot? Do you think I'm not aware of the real cause?'

'Take your drops, then,' said Jakob, holding out the spoon.

'Foxglove,' said Lars, opening his mouth. 'I'm living on flowers.

'The most important things don't need learning,' he went on, propping himself up a little higher on the pillows. 'Breathing, seeing and hearing don't need to be learnt, and that's a shame, because then we set no store by those abilities. Humans are dumb animals who set more store by what's artificial than what's innate; I did it myself and now I'm sorry I wasted so much of my time. I've wasted so much time, Jakob, I've never had sufficient sense of wonder. At our breathing, which carries on by itself when we're asleep or thinking of other things; at our hearts, which beat on and on without tiring. People are inattentive, but that's because they have so many cares. How can they go around rejoicing in the fact that their hearts are beating when all their money's gone and they're on the verge of starvation; anyone who suggests such a thing deserves a beating! And yet it's the only miracle that exists in this world, the fact that we exist.'

'So you think the meaning of life is learning to value it?' said Jakob, thinking of Vogel.

'Don't be so bloody ridiculous,' said Lars in irritation. 'The meaning of life . . . You'll be talking about God next. She's going to ask every single one,' he mumbled, shutting his eyes, 'she won't give up until she's looked them in the face and asked about the boys.' He slid some way down the mountain of pillows and disappeared with a sad grimace, as if he were the one going round searching and questioning and never finding what he sought among the throng.

Once Lars was asleep, Jakob went out to the dining room where his soup stood cooling among the dirty dishes. He piled them up and took the whole lot down to the kitchen. The fire was a glowing mass of embers, and he poured the soup back into the pot and set it to heat while he looked into the little room where Maret sat knitting, one finished stocking on the table in front of her along with a branched candle, and a bun from which she took the occasional bite.

He observed her Christmas celebrations for a while, then ate the salty soup, drank some water from the scoop and took a turn about the courtyard, which lay empty and quiet. The pig's blood still shone through the thin covering of snow. Tobias's window was in darkness, so he pushed the door shut without bolting it and went back up to Lars, who was sleeping with his head in a pool of dark hair, spilling out over the pillow in strange patterns. He pulled up the chair and sat down beside the bed, reached out his hand and filled it with glossy locks that ran through his fingers, locks so unlike his own mat of horsehair. As he looked down at his hand, he found it grotesque beside Lars's thin, dark face and drew it back to hide it between his knees. In the dining room, the clock whirred and then struck hoarsely eleven times with a faint, husky echo.

'You thought I was asleep,' said Lars and smiled, eyes still closed. 'But I didn't want to sleep, I'm listening to the snow. Can you hear how it's got colder? It sounds like someone throwing sand at the window. Lying in a warm bed it's hard to imagine what it feels like to be out there, but one must try and that's what I am doing, trying to imagine what I can't feel. It's cold, it's so cold that it freezes up your nose, and Elisa's going round the men and tapping them on the shoulder, asking her question, moving on to the next one, asking her question, moving on. She's forgetting they're all as frozen as each other and it doesn't really matter who they are. Why is she searching for my brothers? Oh, I should so much like to know what's happening to me!

'But maybe you can tell me,' he went on, opening his eyes, 'now you've tried your hand at anatomy and slit open kings. Can you forgive me for turning inwards, though it's so cold outside and so many people are freezing, and asking you what you think *my* heart looks like? Have I even got one?'

'I think it's a big one.'

'What crap!' shouted Lars. 'It's not big, do you hear; it's small, and shrinking all the time. And since our feelings are in our hearts, I feel less than other people, and now the world is shrinking too, everything's shrinking, all there is left is this room. And that means I must try even harder, I've no time for sleep because I must try to remember exactly *how* it feels when it's so cold your nose freezes up. How does it feel? How cold is the snow when you're lying in it? How cold is the wind?

'Though maybe our feelings are in our eyes instead,' he mumbled, pulling himself into a sitting position. 'Why should the heart always be so important? The eye sees and preserves images, and fortunate are those who have never averted their gaze. Elisa is staring into their faces, but she sees only those who aren't there, what's wrong, what's missing. I've done the same thing, all too often. And then you come along and break the window and ask about the meaning of life as if you weren't good enough to answer yourself. Why did you listen to me and why did I believe I could tell you anything you don't already know? What mires of stupidity; we can't get out of them even in our final moments that are supposed to be so lucid. What strange paths, how they twist and turn. Why did I follow them?'

He had red marks on his cheeks as if someone had slapped him. Suddenly he took Jakob's hand and pulled him close, so Jakob caught the metallic smell of his body and saw the

128

broad strip of sweat on his brow. He tried to reach for the washbowl but as he did so, the grip on his fingers tightened. 'Now you listen,' said Lars in a tinny voice. 'It was wrong but now I know why. It was because I couldn't believe. I lived like a believer but I didn't believe. The clergy talked of a better world, but I saw that world all around me, in *this* world, this world which was admittedly distorted, but not so distorted it was impossible to see how it could have been, how it ought to be, what it could become. There was a film over what I saw, but I thought we'd be able to clear away the film, I thought we'd be able to scrape it off to reveal the ideal, since the ideal was there all the time, hidden by the film but still visible enough for us to be aware of it and think about it and long for it . . . There was no chance of my ever forgetting. Do you see? When I looked about me in the world, it was like the shadow on the wall; it was dark and distorted but still resembled the thing that was casting the shadow: the real world that was there within reach. It's always been within reach, I've always been able to see it; is it so strange then, that I've strained to reach that rather than waiting for eternity? Do you understand me, Jakob? I have no faith, but I've lived as a believer, I've lived in the belief that this world is a distorted reflection of something else, but there is nothing else, no world but this one. I might just as well have lived in it. But I saw only the distortion and that compelled me to try to put it to rights. That was my faith: that it was possible to put everything to rights. But it meant all I saw were the distortions. Do you see, Jakob? Do you understand me?'

'I've never seen the thing you're talking about,' said Jakob. 'I suppose I must only ever have seen the shadow, and simply got used to it.'

Then Lars began all over again, combining his words in new ways and stammering in his impatience at not being able to explain his faith, the faith he wanted to discard. 'For what good is it to me?' he shouted. 'Other people's faith made them easygoing and cheerful, I slept badly at nights. And now all I want to do is lie by the fire and gaze at the sky and listen to the clock, not think about anything. I've never lain in a bed as soft as this before. Could there be a more beautiful sky?'

'I want you to be your usual self,' said Jakob, leaning forward and resting his forehead on the edge of the bed.

'I am afraid that's asking a bit much.'

They heard the whinny of a horse out in the street and the sound of a gate banging shut. 'That'll be Tobias,' said Jakob, sitting up. 'I'm going down to ask him what the hell he means by leaving you alone like this.'

'It's not Tobias, it's the wind. Can't you hear? It's turning to the north-west. I sent him off myself, because I got it into my head that I wanted to be alone. And then I was so glad when you came, so glad that at first I had no idea why I felt the way I did. Then I realised: it's because Jakob's here. You say nothing, you ask nothing, you just break windows and pin up blankets against the draught and build neat little piles of kindling that light instantly. Is it an exercise in patience?'

'I don't know. I don't think so.'

'To live without harming other people . . .' said Lars. 'I wish it were possible.'

Jakob rested his chin in one hand and looked at him. Then he wetted the facecloth and applied it gently to Lars's forehead, removing a strand of hair that had caught at the corner of his mouth; he unbuttoned Lars's shirt and wiped his neck, rubbed his fingertips to try to get rid of the ink that had eaten its way into the skin like tattoos. He dipped the cloth into the water again and wiped it over Lars's lips to give him some of the cool taste he liked so much.

'Are you cold?' he asked and Lars nodded. His eyes, which had been the intense blue of a child's, looked almost black now, with the reflection of the fire like a yellow stain on the dilated pupils. Jakob got up to add more fuel. 'I am sorry to say you won't inherit much,' mumbled Lars behind him. 'Wish there had been more to leave you than a broken clock and an iron pen stand. Maybe the clock can be mended.'

He shifted a little in the bed and coughed. 'Because I assume there's no point in thinking I shall be getting up soon?' he asked, and Jakob, noticing that the wood was reluctant to catch light, took the poker and thrust it into the heap of glowing embers so violently that iron smote stone and smoke billowed out into the room. With his hand shielding his eyes he went over and opened the door to let the smoke out, then turned and saw that Lars was waiting for an answer.

'I don't think so,' he said, and sat down.

He heard himself how hard his voice sounded and saw Lars wince, and realised suddenly that his friend was frightened and distressed, his friend who had always been more the others' friend but was now his, his best friend and the person he wanted to help most of all. It was the first time, for Lars had always seemed unmoved by what befell him, and carefree, as if time were something that had been promised him in unlimited quantities. He had laughed with a kind of scornful ease at his misfortunes and breezed on past them, but now he was sinking and Jakob knew there was no way of saving him. There was nothing he could do for his best friend other than make haste to talk to him or sit quietly if that was what he preferred, give him something to drink and see he kept warm.

It was little enough. But there were no tricks of the trade that could restore this body, this body that was nothing like the other because this one was alive and wanted to go on living. He knew now that it was so: Lars wanted very much to go on living, although there had always been something about him signalling that it was basically all the same to him; but now he wanted to live and his wanting made him ugly, restless, unapproachable, intimidating and pitiful. He clasped Lars's hands as they moved over the sheet, drumming, held them tightly between his own big, coarse hands and said: 'I promise I'll stay with you.'

He could feel the pulse in Lars's wrist, the frightened heart beating beneath his thumb. 'How long, then?' Lars asked.

'Oh,' said Jakob, 'probably not very long. As long as you want. It's not even midnight and I can't go to bed anyway, because I've got to lock up. I'm not sleepy. And tomorrow . . . who knows what will happen then? Nothing will be as it was, Mattias says, but I think things will always stay the same. The soldiers will move off again and we'll all carry on as before.'

'Will you carry on as before, then?' asked Lars, shifting restlessly in the bed. 'Will you go down to the apothecary's shop and unlock the door and fold the counter down? Will Maret stand at the gate and smile at all the passers-by? Will Tobias sit in front of the fire of an evening, perched on the edge of his chair as if he hadn't been invited? Will there still be somebody living in the attic room?'

'Everything will carry on.'

'The swallows under the eaves, the bird cherry, the cargo boats at the entrance to the harbour, the children hunting for driftwood, the cows standing on the edge of the forest in the evening, lowing to be milked. The path to the kitchen door, the steps, Elisa with a book in one hand, setting out the spoons with the other. Will it all carry on?'

'Definitely.'

'Tell me some more.'

'We-ell . . .' said Jakob slowly. 'First, the snow melts. In the north churchyard there are winter aconites and the magpies are clearing out their nests. Then I think we must build a proper set of stairs up to the attic. Mattias will be getting himself a new partner.'

'Will that be you?'

'Certainly not. If he asks I shall say no thank you. Maret has decided she wants a cat, and I expect she can have one. She's going to learn to read this year, and Tobias . . . no, I don't know what I'm going to give him.'

'Tell me some more,' said Lars.

'In the evenings . . . I don't know what happens then. We . . . we go out and sit in the courtyard, under the bird cherry. We're chatting about something. Tobias locks the door to the shop and puts the key in his pocket; he stops to polish his spectacles and looks up at the sky. "It's going to rain," he says.'

'So everything will be just the same?'

'Everything will be nearly the same.'

He fell silent and Lars moved his ice-cold fingers inside Jakob's hand and whispered: 'Go on.'

'I'm too tired,' said Jakob, getting up. 'If I'm to carry on, I must lie down and rest a bit first.' He started unbuttoning his waistcoat, looking down at the slender body shivering under the quilt. 'Lie down, then,' said Lars, turning away his head. 'It's all the same to me. But you said you weren't sleepy.'

'Not sleepy, just tired. And rather cold.'

'Lie down, then,' Lars said again, moving over to make room, and Jakob turned back the quilt and lay down beside him, carefully so as not to rock the bed, then inserted his arm under Lars's neck and pulled his head towards him. 'I'm terribly cold,' he mumbled, clasping Lars's cold, living body with his other arm, holding it bent so as to apply no pressure. 'I walked home with just my shirt on, that was stupid.'

'You're as warm as an oven,' said Lars. 'Now carry on telling me things.'

'I thought we might try making some boiled sweets with aniseed in,' said Jakob, putting two chilled feet between his own. 'Later on in the spring there'll be so much to do with all the things we need to gather. I shall get Tobias to do it, he's good at all that.'

'He knows all about leaves,' said Lars, teeth chattering.

'Leaves and flowers, roots, seeds and berries, he'll make a much better apothecary than I've ever been.'

'Much better. Much.'

'So I suppose you could say everything's turning out for the best,' whispered Jakob, shifting cautiously until they were lying tightly pressed together inside the tangle of sheets.

'Good, for everyone,' said Lars in a strange voice. Jakob leant over him and saw the dreadful sorrow at drifting away into utter loneliness. 'Now it's your turn to tell me things,' he whispered, putting his hand to Lars's cheek. 'Tell me about that other world, the one you saw, the one that was so much better. What would that world have been like? Tell me about it.'

'Soon,' said Lars. 'Just need to rest a while first. Then I'll explain everything.'

He shut his eyes and Jakob lay back down and carefully

held him close, afraid of disturbing or hurting him. His arm had started aching from its uncomfortable position and he thought that was just as well, because it would stop him falling asleep. But he fell asleep even so, and when he awoke the candle had burnt down and the clock had stopped.

CHAPTER 8

He went out into the milky-white dawn and saw a horse lying in the street with its neck extended like a bird in flight. The soldiers were still coming, a thin procession of stragglers emerging from the forest and winding their way across the meadow. He pressed himself flat against the wall, and they passed by without looking at him and without breaking their slow, plodding rhythm. Their clothes hung loose from their emaciated bodies, their hands were wrapped in rags, their swaddled feet were frozen parcels of snow. They did not speak; all that could be heard was the shuffling sound of dogged, exhausted onward movement.

Only one came to a stop, a young man with one arm held up in a sling of bloody bandages. He took a few swaying steps in front of Jakob as if he were dancing, an outlandish dance on feverish, shaking legs before he fell to one side with an exclamation of surprise. Without lifting their eyes from the ground, the others altered their course so as not to tread on him, but Jakob leant forward and looked at his open eyes and the mouth that had stiffened into a sort of smile. He was fair-haired, like so many of them.

An acrid smell of smoke hung over the town, which was unusual this early in the morning. But as he made his way down towards the square he could see that all the big houses had their front gates open, that fires were burning in the courtyards and soldiers were standing or lying around them on straw that had been put down. At hastily erected trestle tables, women were serving soup from steaming kettles, while small children scurried round with bits of bread for the men who stuck out their hands from the folds of their coats and lifted them stiffly to their mouths. A cart rattled by and he had time to see that it was carrying a full load of people, who were being rolled from side to side on the bare boards and lacked the strength to hold on. 'Don't go so fast,' he bawled, but the words were lost in the din and the cart rumbled off towards the hospital in a cloud of snow.

All around him were people running with blankets, fire-wood and bottles of schnapps. Bare-headed women with shawls thrown anyhow round their shoulders jostled with boys pushing handcarts loaded with herring barrels and corn brought up from the warehouses. When the courtyards got too crowded, people moved out into the street and set up new tables by the fires where anything served as fuel: fir cones, torn sacks, broken boxes, mucky straw from the cowsheds. Doors stood open everywhere and the clear boundaries between house, yard and street had evaporated. Skinny horses stood tugging at the straw the men were lying on, or made their own way down to the river.

The empty cart came back from the hospital and Jakob followed it, invisible and purposeless in the scrum. As he approached the square in front of the town hall, the sound issuing from it grew to a roar, as if someone had lifted the place high and given it a shake. The open area was black with people; it was so tightly packed that the carts could make no headway, and the drivers shouted and cracked their whips to make a path through to the steps, where the doctor was standing with his shirtsleeves rolled up. Beside him a number of men lay sprawled in the snow; he was bending over them and beckoning forward the hired hospital hands, who were carrying the bodies to the cart. From inside the town hall, hoarse screams could be heard and a man in a bloody apron stopped in the doorway to shout something to a boy who was struggling to get a cask of schnapps up the steps. The man wiped his red hands and helped him carry in the cask, then the boy took to his heels, running away from the screams, and was gone.

When Jakob went a little closer he could see that skin rugs had been spread out along the town hall wall and the doctor was moving along the row of recumbent men, sorting them. He unwound a bandage and examined a blue-black foot, attempted to shake some life into a moaning man who lay curled up on his side with his knees drawn up, pulled another into a sitting position against the wall and forced some schnapps into him, studied a swollen hand that was held out for inspection. The frostbite victims were helped into the town hall and those who were delirious with fever or unconscious were loaded on to the carts and driven away. The schnapps got others on their feet again and they tottered off of their own accord to look for a bed and some food. More men were coming in all the time, dragging one another or supporting themselves on sticks they had broken off in the forest. It was the old and the very young who were arriving last. None of them bore weapons.

Now he was aware of the smell that surrounded them, the chokingly sweet smell of rotten flesh. 'Quick, grab him,' came a yell in his ear, and he turned round and tried to catch a falling body that slid through his grasp and sank down in a heap on the ground. It was a boy, fifteen at most,

swiftly they had to provide them with warmth, food and a place to sleep, for that was the only way to avoid seeing the wretched state to which they had all been reduced, devastated and diminished into shaking boys with fevered eyes, freezing in the snow and calling for water. It was not sympathy that made the townspeople rush, but the fear of something worse, not thoughts but automatic reflexes.

A town of two thousand inhabitants had had a few days and nights to study a swarm of high-status guests, who in their anxieties about political upheavals and the accession of a new monarch had held a vigil over the remains of a king. Now the guests would be leaving and they would be on their own with what was left: a thousand ragged men without proper shoes, who were far from home and hardly still had feet to walk on. Without sympathy, with cold faces, the townspeople lifted up those who fell and supported them; they ladled pork and root vegetables into wooden bowls, they put mildewed old quilts from their attics to air in front of the fire, they left their beds and gave away their clothes. The intense concentration induced by hurry and necessity made every face the same, so they became an army advancing around the small points of grey stillness that were the soldiers.

But he himself had no allotted task. He had lain in the warehouse and dreamt of being on board a ship; now he was standing on some steps and still had no part in what was happening because it was not happening to him. Nothing had happened to him, and what he could see was as unreal as the dream of the creaking timbers of new wood and the wind whining in the rigging. And yet he saw it all, he felt it all and heard it all: the screams from the town hall, the crying of the boy, the smell of dead body parts, the hiss of the cauterising iron, the doctor roaring out his orders in an ever hoarser voice, Leo Fahlgren resting on his stick at a street corner, his wisps of grey hair blowing in the wind. Sofie was standing on a carriage from which the horses had been unhitched, dispensing schnapps in dainty little birthday glasses which were quickly drained and passed back to be refilled. She was red in the face, as utterly composed as everyone else, and so intent on not spilling a drop that she did not see him although he was standing only a few metres away. 'Drive on,' shouted the doctor, and yet another cart lumbered off with its load of sick soldiers. An old man fell headlong towards the fire and was quickly hauled aside by two silent women who had hitched up their skirts for greater freedom of movement.

He heard the crunch of an axle breaking as a cart went into a pothole. He was also the first to see the spiral of wind that came swirling up from the sea to shroud the square in smoking snow, making the soldiers huddle up and moan as if recalling something terrible. Leo Fahlgren covered his face with his arm and stumped over to a man who was wrapped in his coat and leaning against a wall, asleep; he woke him with a poke of his stick and offered him his hip flask. The playful wind took a last sweep around the square, smacked into gates, overturned a table and snatched up some straw before it rushed on by, leaving the fine-grained snow to fall in a powdery coating over firewood, food, clothes, animals and people. A little girl laughed and caught a hat in mid-air, but was restrained by a woman who gave her a shake and dragged her off through the crowds.

It was extremely cold. The sky was pale red with a tired sun hanging from the clock tower, quivering like a water droplet; the trees were empty of birds and the river was freezing over again. Some dogs foraging for scraps among

141

the tables sniffed greedily at the men lying along the wall of the town hall and were chased off by a snowball from the doctor. His normally so ruddy face was as grey as paper, and suddenly he crumpled on to the steps with a thud and slept for a few minutes until one of the hired hospital hands shook him, forced him to his feet and dragged him off to the passageway at the cellar entrance, where a man half covered in snow sat overlooked in the shelter of a barrel. Seeing how exhausted they were, Jakob went down the steps to the passageway, lifted the man on to his shoulder like a sack and tipped him on to the back of the cart. When he turned round, the doctor had already returned to the sick soldiers; he was squatting in the snow, lifting an eyelid with his thumb. 'Out of the way, please,' croaked someone beside Jakob, and an old man in a broad-brimmed hat interlocked his hands to make a stirrup for a shivering boy, who was swung up on to the back of the cart and huddled down on a little bit of hay. The driver cracked his whip and the cart moved off, jolted over a pile of snow and grazed close by a man who made no attempt to jump aside and was spun round by the impact to face the other way. He stood with his arms wrapped round his body and looked straight into fresh air, oblivious to the fact that the view had suddenly changed. A wooden pole had torn a hole in his thin uniform jacket, and Jakob took off his coat and put it round his shoulders.

For his part, he felt warm; the wind that was blowing in new gusts had no effect on him. In the road, two men were arguing beside the broken cart; he went over and lifted it out of the pothole, surprised at his own strength. From here there was a view of the slope up to the church and the officers who had assembled there ready for departure, a gathering quite different from that down in the square. He looked at his hands, which were bleeding but did not hurt, and wiped them clean in the snow while the men went on arguing; then he headed diagonally over the open square, kicked the ring of half-burnt branches round the fire into the centre, pulled up a boy who had fallen to his knees in the snow and brushed his trousers, went into the yard of a house he did not know, into a kitchen he did not know and drank some water from a cup. Nobody addressed him, nobody saw him. He stood by the window and looked at a girl feeding some liquid to an old man, who was gripping her wrist and trying to keep his head still. Jakob drank a little more water and went back out. The boy was down on his knees again and a bare-headed man with soiled clothes draped the boy's arm round his shoulders and dragged him along towards the town hall. When Jakob went over to help, he realised that the dirty man was Mattias and that Mattias was looking straight at him without recognising him, while talking loudly into the boy's ear and trying to make him move his feet by kicking them. One of the surgeon's hired hands came out and threw an armful of bloody rags on to the fire. From the slope up to the church came loud cries and a chorus of voices, all shouting in unison: 'Yes!'

Jakob turned his back on it all and headed off, away from the cries, the stench, the racket of iron-rimmed wheels, the billowing yellow smoke, the rags and the crack of whips. He went down to the river and tramped along the ice, which was closing over the water and was blue and full of air bubbles, past the straw-roofed huts that were sagging under the snow and had windows the size of the palm of a hand, past the cooking fires, the goats nibbling on osier twigs, the dungheaps and latrine pits; he went along by the ships with the lovely names, frozen into the water but moving in ways imperceptible to the eye yet still audible – like a soft rustle when the tide came in, as the salt water streamed under the ice, a soft scraping of wood against wood, a rhythmic chiming as the iron rings on the quayside were lifted and fell again. *Hope, Joy, Fortune Seeker, Pamiras, Balder* and *Admiral.* He did not stop. He had the sun at his back, a cold white sun with no strength to cast shadows. Out in the meadow, a horse was up to its belly in crusted snow; when he whistled it raised its front legs in a feeble effort to get free.

He did not stop, nor did he turn and look back, for now the town had to disappear. The bridge leading up to the wooden quays was slippery with hard-packed, trampled snow; the plundered warehouses had a pungent smell of salt herring and split dried cod. He went on past them. At the end of the row stood his own, where he had slept among the stacks of planks long ago, four days ago, until Mattias came and woke him up. The only things he could hear were his footsteps and his breathing, and he listened in surprise to his own sounds, stamped his feet to intensify them, called out over the water and waited for the echo which came back sharp and clear in the cold air. He talked to himself. He put his hands to his mouth like a funnel and called to himself, then heard himself answer in a deep voice from the hill on the far side of the harbour entrance.

He had reached the end of the quay so he jumped down into the snow, which lay more sparsely the further out towards the blowy sea he went, and was criss-crossed by delicate, secret tracks, not like those leading from the harbour to the town. It was as if birds had been hopping around below the quays and searching for food on the shoreline, so winding were the tracks and so small the feet that had made them. He took care not to spoil them as he walked, because he found them beautiful, like garlands of flowers painted on a cupboard or the lines on the palm of a hand.

He could see the cliffs now, and the water between them was the colour of tin, with black stripes where the wind ruffled it. The town was gone, the only sounds out here were of the seabirds, the wind and the slow swell rustling in the ice. He followed the tracks until they disappeared into the heather, skidded down an icy, sloping rock and landed in the sand, which had been swept clean by the waves and was hard beneath his feet. The boulders along the shoreline had collars of flaky ice, but the water was still open with a thin white smoke on the surface that went whirling up with each gust of wind. Soon it would freeze over, the inner bays were already syrupy with icy slush that rattled against the rock walls. It would be a long time until *Hope* and *Admiral* could cast off their moorings and sail for England with timber and iron.

He walked north because he wanted to get further away, so far away that there was nothing left but water and salt air, white light and silence. Never again did he want to see the confusion of cramped little houses or the façade of the town hall, the church tower, the expanse of meadow beyond the town gate where they had waited for the dead King and his entourage, the street, the steps up to the attic, the clock in the dining room, the bed pulled up to the fire, the window he had broken open or the view from the window. There was no way for him to escape all that, but he wanted to postpone seeing it again for as long as possible, walk straight ahead and not think about anything but what he was seeing, which was beautiful and quite disconnected from all that was happening a few kilometres inland, clean and beautiful things like icicles, frost flowers, snow crystals, dried seed heads, bleached bone and dead trees.

The black seaweed stood out against white sand, the cliffs were striped with ribbons of quartz, the gulls shredded the air with swooping cuts, the islands turned blue in the hazy sun. Out here you could call and no one would hear, the sound would vanish and leave no evidence of ever having existed. He trod on a coral-coloured crab shell and crushed it, cast a stone that splintered through the brittle ice, climbed a hill and found a new bay, exactly like the one he'd just left: the same red tongues of rock enclosing a little beach, the same rounded stones on the waterline and twisted ropes of seaweed. There had been a building there once: the foundations and the remains of a stone jetty could still be seen. Beyond the jetty, in a hollow sheltered by a high rock wall and carpeted with shells, he saw the children.

There were five of them. He recognised them from the cellar, where they had been given lessons in worldly wisdom and eaten gruel while Lars Björnson read them 'The Fox and the Grapes', 'The Boy who Cried Wolf' and 'The Dog in the Manger'. Two boys and three girls who were jumping from rock to rock and poking about in the snow with sticks, hunting for whatever turned up. They arranged their finds in piles on the beach: bits of plank, bottles, ends of rope, posts from jetties uprooted by the autumn gales, rags, huge shells knobbly with acorn barnacles. Two of the girls were filling a sack with seaweed and the elder boy was trying to salvage a log that was bobbing just beyond the edge of the ice.

The children were alert, they were bold and noisy, shouting to each other and jealously guarding their belongings. One of the girls had a clouded eye from having fallen over in the street with a milk bottle and got a splinter of glass in it. She was wrapped in a huge shawl that had belonged to some-body else; it was tied at the back and pulled tight over arms that were blue with cold. They were a ragged lot, dressed in patches, their clogs stuffed with straw and their hands bare. They moved with practised ease over the beach, lifting chunks of ice with their sticks to see what lay hidden underneath them, efficiently discarding anything that could not be used as fuel or in some other way; yet at the very next moment they could not resist keeping a wing-quill or a bit of green glass whose only function was that you could hold it up to the light and look at it.

They gathered with interest around a dead seagull and poked at its outstretched wings, then scampered on to a clump of lyme-grass with their sacks dangling behind them. They were like dry leaves whirling in the wind, five little skeletons, whistling and fighting over a piece of torn fishing net. The girl with the blind eye bent forward as she walked, her head cocked like a thrush listening for worms. Whenever she found anything she liked, she held it up to her face and scrutinised it before quickly putting it into a cloth bag that was tied round her waist with a rope.

He stood at the edge of the beach looking at them, but all his thoughts were with Lars Björnson, who had been cut off in mid-sentence and had never had time to explain what the real world was like, the one that cast the shadow in which they all lived, the world he said was so unlike this one but still within reach. Jakob could not see the shadow, he could only see the children living their lives, the birds living theirs, the changing sea that could not grow any more real than it was, the pale sky. The birds dived for food, the children hunted for wood. He had never managed to finish his conversation with Lars but he knew that a shadow, however dark it may be and however distorted, always bears a resemblance to whatever is casting it, all the same.

147

CHAPTER 9

The little horse did not want to move. Jakob had untangled the reins that were caught round its front legs, but when he tried to pull the horse forward, it dug its hooves into the ground and put its head down like a bull. It was a pathetic creature, thin and unkempt, with raw white patches where the harness had rubbed and a face as knotted as an old tree stump. Jakob tugged on the reins and tried to remember the right words for encouraging an exhausted horse through deep snow, but it was only when he let go and went to stand at the horse's head that it stopped its wilful protest and threw itself forward, puffing and blowing. With harelike leaps it plunged across the meadow and out into the road where it stopped for a moment, trembling after its exertion, while Jakob, catching up with it, talked into its great hairy ear and stroked its legs, which were torn and bleeding from the abrasive crust of the snow. When he walked on, the horse trotted obligingly after him, up through the poorest part of town where the air was heavy with the dinner-time smell of putrid herring.

He liked the feel of the animal keeping close and snorting its warm breath down his back. He had knotted the reins and placed them over the horse's back, but it still went on following him. Each time he turned round, its eyes were there, friendly behind their white lashes, and he scratched the tousled crown of its head and spoke softly while the horse shut its eyes and rubbed its chin against his shoulder. Its teeth were quite badly worn down. He gave its neck one final hearty slap and went on up the hill, and the next time he turned round it was gone, enticed into a backyard where a little girl was throwing down hay from the loft for some sheep. He was on his own again, in an alley which had acted as a tunnel for the wind, piling the snow into enormous drifts against the walls of the houses so there was only a narrow passage left to walk through.

When he came out on to the street he could hear the lantern blowing to and fro in the wind, squeaking on its rusty hook over the tavern door, and he pushed open the door and went down the steps into the warmth from the open fire, the crowd of men sitting round it, the bottles and glasses glinting on the tables, the landlord standing behind the counter knocking the tap out of a barrel of beer. He was back where he had started, in the comforting company of unfamiliar people who did not even look up when he ordered his schnapps and took it with him to the furthest table in the darkest corner; the comforting presence of indifferent people who left him in peace yet still kept him company with their murmur and the sight of their backs. He filled his glass, drank and felt the wonderful, dizzying sensation that rose from his empty stomach to be instantly transformed into warmth in his fingers. Leaning back against the wall, he prepared himself to forget everything except the dizziness, the warmth, the burning taste in his mouth, the gentle buzz of voices that gradually faded until he was sitting alone, alone with the glass warming his hands.

The thick walls shut out every sound, and time vanished

into the early dusk. In here, there was nothing: no rush, no agitation, no reminders. He stretched his legs out in front of him and felt the warmth and the alcohol making him soft and accommodating. If everything was still in full swing outside those walls it was none of his business any more, but perhaps it had all been quietening down, just as he had. Perhaps evening had come. Perhaps the people were already asleep in the dark town, while he sat here alone in the circle of light from a badly dipped candle with a faltering, sputtering flame. If he were to decide to go out, he might find that the streets were empty, the houses bolted and barred for the night, resting in a thick, heavy silence broken only by the sleepy sound of the trampling animals in the outbuildings, which would last through till morning when the maids broke the ice in the pails and blew on the embers. But no soldiers, no dead horses, no boys in the snow, no commotion up by the church, no changes in his house. He would willingly hand the house over to those who were living there, if they would only promise not to change. For himself, he would be content just to catch sight of them sometimes from the courtyard; he would ask nothing more as long as they were there, all of them, with no one missing. There was to be no one missing. He poured more drink from the bulbous bottle, spilt some and laughed at his own hand that could do so many things but not manage to hold a glass steady. 'You're a filthy pig,' muttered a voice out of the darkness beside him, and since the warmth had made him drowsy and inclined to honesty, he obediently answered, 'Yes.'

He could not even be sure there was anything at all outside the walls. Perhaps he was the sole survivor, locked in a capsule of darkness along with the whining voice scolding him from the shadows, and no doubt with every justification. Perhaps he was just as much alone as he had felt himself to be, but now he did not care. These last days he had gone back and forth, to and fro across the town, without resting or thinking or even knowing why he was doing what he had been asked to do, but now he had finally sat down, and a scolding was a small price to pay for the deep well of rest and oblivion that had opened up for him here, two metres below ground level and disguised as a tavern with the help of some tables and an improvised counter.

'A filthy pig,' said the ice-grey voice, 'a dumb beast with no brains and no discretion, a lazy ox who lets a child do his job while he hides from his wife, a coward who takes a blow and gives none in return, a bad businessman and a bad friend, a useless horseman, ungifted in every possible way. Hardly worth having when you think about it, the way he's handled things, made a mess of most of them; in fact, you could say he's been a failure at everything he's done in his life. Isn't that so, Jakob Törn?'

'It certainly is,' said Jakob, wiping the table with his hand.

'And a drunkard, I forgot to mention that; the kind that loses control and disgraces himself and starts lashing out at defenceless old folk. An unusually sorry sight, that Jakob Törn! And he had such prospects, too, the best start you could wish for, a really nice boy once upon a time, who could have been a good person. Not that he's exactly bad now, I don't mean to say that, but not good enough, not as good as he might have been. And now he's going to find out what it's like, because now no one needs him any more. They've managed by themselves for so long that they've learnt to cope without him. How must that make him feel?'

'Not as bad as you might think.'

'Oh yes, he could die on the spot and the world would

carry on very nicely all the same. It must make him a little bitter, really.'

'No, it doesn't,' Jakob said, turning towards the corner where the man sat huddled on a bench, talking into the wall. 'I'm not afraid of disappearing, you're all welcome to forget me. I don't want other people to disappear, it's true, but myself I wouldn't mind just getting up and being gone without trace. What does it matter? What's the use of the traces when the person is gone?'

'Oh, you're such a liar!' said the man, swinging round suddenly. 'You're talking a load of rot, because you know perfectly well how carefully we preserve the traces when they're all we've got left, preserve them more lovingly than we do the living, and never give up trying to follow them. Just look at yourself now, as red-eyed as a tearful child; is it the dead hero you're grieving for or those poor devils out there in the snow? Or is it your friend, that miserable piece of work who never did anything more useful than sit and poke away with a pen? A friend who gets into bed with your wife the minute you turn your back isn't worth grieving over. Go and bury him in the dung pit instead. At least that way he'll be of some use.'

'It's time you held your tongue, Wessman,' said Jakob, rubbing his eyes. 'I'm sorry for what happened at the Mayoress's party, but you needn't think it gives you leave to say whatever you like.'

'Oh but I will, though,' said Wessman, pulling his chair up to the table so the light fell on his ugly face and the greasy woollen wig drooping lopsidedly over one ear. 'I can say whatever I like tonight, because you wouldn't dare do it again. And I *will* say what I like, whatever I feel the need to say. Since I, unlike my old friend Leo Fahlgren, take no pleasure in that spectacle down in the square, I'm obliged to sit here and talk to you if I want company. And I do.'

'You want *what?*' asked Jakob in bewilderment, waking slowly from a rest which had been deep and midnight blue but could not survive the other man's intrusive prattle.

'I want company,' said Wessman sulkily, reaching for the bottle. 'Come to think of it, maybe you're grieving for yourself. Can't be much fun knowing you're a filthy pig.'

He filled both their glasses and drained his own at once, generous now he was drinking at someone else's expense. He appeared to be measuring the contents of the bottle and weighing it up against his own inebriated state and what he could see of Jakob's; then he filled his glass again and drew it towards him. 'You can't just stop doing things,' he said indistinctly.

Jakob leant over the table and looked at him. 'Can't you?' he asked amiably, holding out the candle so Wessman could light his pipe.

'No, you can't. Look at me traipsing round to Leo's house every blessed evening, even though we have such an abysmally boring time together. The same old harping on about how it used to be, the same old stories we've told a thousand times before. One talks and the other one thinks about something else, then we swap and then we swap back again. Then we both sit in silence and stare at the fire until his daughter comes in with the coffee and is just as fed up, with the old man's carping and everything she has to do for him, the food she cooks and he complains about, always the same old moans about some bloody soup he's longing for. But do you think he can remember what was in it? The same stories that are half lies and half faulty memory and the same old self-pity: if only this and *that* hadn't happened, everything would have been different and then I would have been a rich man, a great man, I would, yes indeed I would. If only this and *that* hadn't happened. By the end we're so bored we can hardly sit upright any more, and then we decide that's it, that's finally it, and we say goodbye for ever; but the next evening there we are again, the same fire, the same old men chewing over that time, that accursed time, and how it would have been if *that* hadn't happened, that thing nobody can remember any longer. We can't stand each other, but it doesn't mean we give up. And d'you know why?'

'I haven't the faintest idea.'

'Because you never stop hoping. You think: maybe today he'll have something new to say, maybe today something unexpected will happen, today he might surprise me by saying something other than what I think he will. And then maybe I shall surprise myself and tell him something amazingly interesting he's never heard the like of. You don't stop hoping, and even if he's just the same as ever, because he always is, his daughter really does occasionally happen to be less surly, gives him a little pat as she goes past and says, "Would you like a cushion under your foot, Papa?" Or she's made something nice to offer us, something with sugar. You never know, the possibility does exist . . .

'It's the same thing here,' he went on, moving closer so Jakob was aware of the pungent smell of dirty clothes, bad teeth, age and loneliness. 'A man can come and sit in here, drink cheap spirits and look round, just in case there's anybody he doesn't know, somebody to talk to who wouldn't exactly cheer him up but might at least be disagreeable and stupid in a novel way. And while he's waiting for that to happen, at least it's warm in here, he can hear voices and see faces around him. There are people here and we need people, but you don't understand that people need to be with other people if they want to stay human, because you're like a bear in the forest.'

'So you're claiming to be more human than me, are you?'

Wessman raised his glass and sniffed it suspiciously, then tipped his head back and drank. 'I don't think it makes any odds,' he said hoarsely, thumping his chest. 'It's not a competition, is it? Just as long as you've grasped the principle.'

He leant back on his chair and disappeared behind a curtain of dirty yellow smoke. Through the tiny window above his head the street was visible, and the feet of some men marching by. Wessman puffed on his pipe, cleared his throat, spat on the floor and blew his nose on his sleeve before exhaling a new mouthful of smoke in Jakob's face. With his wide mouth, his powerful jaw and colourless little eyes, Wessman looked like an anglerfish, an ugly, warty fish lying in the mud on the bottom, waiting for its prey. He choked with silent laughter as Jakob coughed on the smoke and then gestured to the landlord to bring another bottle. 'Aren't you going to say something now?' he asked, when he had poured some drink and put the bottle down on the floor beside him. 'You can always tell old Wessman he's a shit if you don't want to say anything about yourself.'

'I haven't got anything to say about myself.'

'Well, why ever not? There are times when anyone might think you were asleep, you're so quiet. Is that it? Are you asleep, Jakob Törn? You can talk to me, because I don't give a damn about your feelings; you needn't worry about confiding in me, anything you like, because I won't be listening anyway. And if I should happen to hear something, I'll have forgotten it by the end of the day, you're so unimportant.' Suddenly he slammed his hand down on to the table and roared: 'Now I really do think it's your turn to say something. Say something, Jakob Törn, you've been holding your tongue long enough.'

Jakob drained his glass. Then he said: 'I can't talk to my friend, because he's dead.'

Someone had opened the door to the street and an icy wind blew in between the tables and wound itself round their legs. 'Don't stand there dithering!' shouted Wessman to an old man dressed in mourning who had not managed to shut the door quickly enough, and was coming down the stairs with a cloud of snow in his wake.

'I can't talk to my friend,' Jakob said again. 'He's dead.'

'I heard,' said Wessman. 'But why let a little thing like that get in the way? My dear little wife, who was too good and noble for this world, left it seven years ago, but that doesn't mean I've stopped engaging her in conversation. There's no need for such inconstancy, no excuse for such unfaithful behaviour. She doesn't answer, but the gods know it's not the first time, for though she was a dear little lady, she had her tiresome moods. She could stop talking for days on end when something wasn't to her liking, and you had to keep at it. Sure enough, she'd always thaw out in the end.'

'But it still isn't the same thing,' Jakob said. 'You surely wouldn't have me believe she's just been sulking for seven years and is going to answer you any day now? Let's stop this game; what's gone is gone for ever and what we didn't manage to say in time is dead. He's gone, I won't get to talk to him again. There's just silence, he doesn't exist.'

'Well, you don't know everything,' said Wessman sullenly. 'And I don't intend giving up talking to my dear wife just because she isn't sitting beside me listening. I fill in the answers myself, because I know more or less what she'd say.

No, I know *exactly* what she'd say. Now you can't call that silent and dead, can you, when I've got her voice in here in my head?'

'I don't know what to call it,' said Jakob. 'Better than nothing, I suppose.'

'I should say it is! But you haven't got a voice because you haven't kept at it like I have. And no one's got your voice either, because you're not worth the bother. You haven't bothered to be worth anyone else's bother.'

'What rubbish,' Jakob said wearily. 'What the hell do you know about me? We don't know each other, you're only sitting here so you don't have to pay for your own drink.'

'And as for those traces,' said Wessman, slurring his words, 'the ones you say don't exist, in my house they're everywhere and that's why I don't let anyone in. Except old Leo, but he has to sit in the kitchen. I won't let anyone trample on the traces of my dear little wife and spoil them.'

'What do they look like then, the traces?' asked Jakob, reaching under the table for the bottle that was wedged for safekeeping between the other man's legs.

'You wouldn't understand them,' said Wessman contentedly. 'You wouldn't even see them, they're only for me. That's the secret: for the traces to be seen, there has to be someone following them. I expect yours are like bear tracks in the snow that get covered over or melt away; nobody bothers to follow them. There has to be somebody following them, then you can see them, then they stay where they are.'

'Somebody following them?'

'That's right,' said Wessman sleepily, resting his arms on the dirty table. 'Somebody, anybody, following the tracks.' He gave a hoarse laugh and whispered: 'Watch out for the hunter, Jakob, he's got a gun.'

'It's time for you to go home,' Jakob said.

'Go home,' rambled Wessman, 'home to my dear little wife. Then there'll be a row; she can be harsh. But all the same . . .'

'What?'

'All the same I feel so happy when she scolds me.'

He reached out a hand for his glass, knocked it over, tittered as the schnapps spilt into Jakob's lap and then slumped forward, his forehead resting on his folded arms. 'So happy when she shouts and screams,' he mumbled, 'just as happy as when she's nice. If she's shouting I can hear all the better how much she likes me. She's just glad I'm home, or cross, it doesn't matter which. It's all the same in her case, strong feelings in that dear old bag of bones. Makes me feel so important when she carries on like that.'

'Time you went home,' said Jakob sternly, shaking the other man's arm which was lying in a puddle of schnapps.

'Not at all,' shouted Wessman, suddenly sitting bolt upright, his face a blotchy red with a white mark on the cheek where it had been pressed against the edge of the table. 'It's you who should go home and stay there, it's high time if you don't want it all to go to rack and ruin. Not that I give a damn anyway, you go to hell, makes no odds. Oh, how we shall laugh as Jakob Törn sells his last shirt at a bankruptcy auction. Will you build yourself a little boat afterwards and go herring fishing? And the Mayor too, and everyone else in this damned town; the whole lot of you can build boats. You'll get no help from me.'

'Time for you to go now, Wessman,' said the landlord, coming over to their table and taking hold of the old man, who puffed himself up, lashed out with his arms and then collapsed, suddenly compliant and maudlin. 'You're all so kind to me,' he sobbed, patting Jakob's arm. The landlord led him from the table, put his hat on his head and sent him off up the steps with a gentle push. At the door Wessman turned and called: 'Jakob Törn should go home, too.'

'He probably should,' the landlord called back, 'but not until he's paid his bill. A small fortune, the way you've been knocking it back. You old tosspot.'

'I'll pay,' said Jakob, getting to his feet. He put some coins on the counter and hurried up the steps, but when he came out into the street Wessman had disappeared into the grey twilight that was draped so softly and beautifully over the houses you might imagine it was any ordinary Christmas afternoon, with people on their way home to roaring fires and tables spread with food, which was why they were in such a hurry. He stood still in the crush and could smell the sharp smell of snow, more snow in the clouds that were massing over the mountain. A single star in the pale sky, fiery red streaks where the sun was going down. A woman knocked into him and dropped her basket, and he helped her retrieve the contents: a piece of pork, two candles tied together with string, coffee in a twist of paper and a little packet of tobacco. The woman ran off without thanking him. He stuck his hands in his pockets and leant against the wall, for unlike her he was not on his way home. Around him the stream of people was thinning out, the street was emptying and the last front doors were shutting. At the bottom of the hill he caught sight of Tobias, traipsing towards him with a knapsack over his shoulder.

He recognised him from his way of keeping close to the buildings, as if he were afraid of getting lost. His misted spectacles were two blind discs directed at the ground and his clothes were sooty, as if he had spent the night by an open fire.

'What on earth do you look like?' called Jakob, and the boy stopped and peered in puzzlement through the grey light. Then he saw who it was calling him and came reluctantly over to Jakob's side of the street, rubbing his spectacles on his chest.

'What do you look like yourself?' he mumbled, putting the side pieces of his spectacles back over his ears.

'What do you mean by that?'

'That you don't look yourself. But perhaps I've just forgotten.'

'It hasn't been that long, has it?' said Jakob.

'Hasn't it?' said Tobias morosely. 'I can't remember exactly, and it doesn't matter anyway. I haven't got time to stand here and discuss it.'

'Wait a minute,' said Jakob, grabbing his arm, but the boy pulled free and went on doggedly, up the street. He had never behaved like that before. Jakob went after him, and as he came abreast of Tobias he heard him talking to himself: 'One left,' he said under his breath, 'got to get rid of the last one.'

'What are you talking about?' Jakob asked, falling into step beside the boy, who was stumbling through the snow clutching on to the empty knapsack as if for support.

'I can't go home otherwise,' said Tobias. 'Promised to hand them all out, promised faithfully.'

'Listen,' said Jakob sternly, taking him in his arms and turning him round, 'you just stand still, or I shall be very angry. What are you doing here, muttering? And why did you run off and leave everything yesterday evening? The notary is dead.'

'I know,' said Tobias. 'That's why I can't go back home. Got to find somebody . . .'

'Yes?' said Jakob, shaking him.

161

'Find somebody to give this last leaflet to.'

He stood there swaying in Jakob's grasp, as thin as a blade of grass, his eyes roving behind their spectacle lenses as he scanned the gloomy street where the first candles were already being lit in the windows.

'They've all gone home,' said Jakob, carefully loosening his hold. 'You can give me the last one.'

'I don't know if that counts,' said the boy, kicking at the snow.

'But what if I'd be really glad to have one?'

'That makes no difference, I'm afraid.'

He pulled off the knapsack and held it up in front of Jakob. 'I've already handed out two hundred and forty-nine,' he went on, 'but I've been very discriminating. If all you wanted was to get rid of them you could just toss them in a heap in the square. But I searched out all the places where they'd do the most good, and it took me all night. Now I've only got one left. I promised Lars I wouldn't come home until I'd finished.'

'You can give it to me,' Jakob said.

When the boy made no answer he took the knapsack from him, opened it and took out a sheet of paper covered in writing. The heading was in bold capital letters. He held up the sheet of paper and turned it to find an angle where there was enough light, but the text ran together in a blur and all he could see was the big blue words along the top: 'Thoughts on the Abolition of Dictatorship and a New World.' The flourish that underlined them ended in a blot, as if the pen had pierced the paper and stuck fast. 'Oh, all right,' said Tobias from behind him, 'you'd better take it, then. I suppose one more or less won't matter.'

'What is this?' Jakob asked, running his finger along the

lines. Once his eyes had adjusted he could make out a few words: *Earth*, *betrayed*, *hunger*, *king*, *people*, *assembly*, *right* and *new*.

'Can't you see? It's a fairy tale.'

'Seems a bloody peculiar fairy tale to me. What's it about? Who's read it?'

'Oh, everybody,' said Tobias. 'Nearly everybody.' He peered down into the knapsack, shook it as if to assure himself it was empty, then put it back on his shoulder. 'The abolition of dictatorship,' he mumbled, 'that's what it's about. And a new world. I went up towards the church first, like he said I should, and then handed out the rest down at the square. It's such thick paper, people can share. I gave the officers one between three.'

He was almost his old self again. When Jakob lifted him by the collar, flung him forward and then began dragging him up towards the apothecary's shop, he went submissively, as if he had no objection to the hand that was tugging and shaking him. 'Officers,' shouted Jakob, 'are you so flaming stupid that you go round showing a thing like this to the King's men? Ruddy brat, you must be weak in the head.'

'You needn't worry,' said Tobias breathlessly, 'nobody ever sees me and they wouldn't have harmed me anyway. We're living in different times now.'

'Oh yes?' shouted Jakob. 'Is that what you think?'

'That was what he said. Jakob, you needn't worry.'

'What the hell would I have to worry about? But as for you, I'm going to lock you in the attic and leave you there until they've gone, every last one. Hah! So that was what he said, that we're living in different times now. And you believed him?'

He suddenly loosened his grip and Tobias overbalanced

and fell on to all fours. 'I think Lars was right,' said the boy, shaking off the snow. 'Don't you?'

'No, I don't,' Jakob replied, looking down at Tobias's head which was dark with moisture. 'I think everything will carry on exactly as before. It always does. If anyone asks we'll just have to say you've run away.'

'I'm not going to run away,' said Tobias, getting up. 'And I'm not going to stay in the attic either. Why shouldn't times be able to change like anything else?'

'Times never change. And if they do, it won't be on account of a few bits of paper you've been running round handing out.'

'Odd,' said Tobias with a little laugh, 'that was exactly what Lars thought you'd say.'

'Oh he did, did he? And what did you say to that?'

'I said he was wrong,' said Tobias quietly.

They had stopped outside the entrance to the courtyard and the apothecary's shop. There was no sign of the man who had been lying there that morning, and the horse lay hidden under a snowdrift that had erased the contours of the great body, leaving something soft and white, glittering and beautiful. Jakob looked at the pitiful boy, who without a vestige of ill will in his thin face stood trembling beside him like a frightened dog, attempting to brush the lumps of snow from his trouser legs. 'So you used to talk to Lars?' he said in surprise and tried to imagine it: the man and the boy and the room where they sat, the rustle of paper, the scratch of the pen, the secret words flying between them as feather-soft as shuttlecocks.

'We talked,' whispered the boy, 'we talked all night sometimes. He said so many things, and I remember every word, I remember everything. Everything.'

'That is a lot,' said Jakob with a smile.

'And I always will.'

It began to snow again, big, light flakes that caught in their eyelashes and tickled their lips. Jakob was still holding the piece of blue paper in his hand.

'Aren't you going to read it?' the boy asked.

At that he folded up the paper and slipped it inside his shirt. He took hold of the door handle and said: 'I shall read it later.'

CHAPTER 10

There was no one in the house, but they could hear foot-steps and voices through the wall adjoining the apothecary's shop. 'I swear I locked it,' cried Tobias, running after Jakob back across the courtyard and up the steps to the rear door. 'The key's in my pocket, I can show you if you want.' A thin wedge of lamplight fell on the floor of the little office where Jakob had spent so many evenings, and in the shop itself seven strange men were standing in a row against the wall while Maret spread straw and empty sacks on the rough floorboards. At the other end of the room, Elisa stood watching with her back pressed against the front door and a pile of blankets in her arms, but when Jakob came in she dropped them, slipped softly under the countertop and vanished into the alcove where he stored the drugs in a tall wooden cabinet. He could hear her breathing in there in the dark as she pulled out drawers and moved bottles as if she had some knowledge of their contents. 'There'll be pillows, too,' said Maret, shaking out the blankets, 'but we haven't had time to stuff them yet.' 'We don't need pillows,' said one of the men, and fumbled to pull off his shoes.

Beside him, a boy whose face was flushed with fever slid down the wall and crawled over to a bed. He lay down on his side and pulled up the blanket, his hands like a white knot under his chin. The other men moved slowly in the confined space, took off their knapsacks, unbuckled their belts, then sat down on the dusty straw as if waiting for something.

'It's cold in here,' said Jakob in a low voice. 'We'd better go downstairs and light a fire in the baking oven.'

'We already have,' said Maret, who had brought a big pot from the kitchen and was ladling porridge into bowls for Tobias to hand round. 'The fire's been alight for an hour. There's another man in the notary's room, but he'll be dead soon.'

There was a noise from the darkness behind them, an abrupt scream of protest like when a cat gets shut in a door, and a bottle fell to the floor and smashed. 'What's wrong with saying that?' said Maret, looking round. 'You know he's delirious. He was already raving when they carried him in.'

'It's true, young mistress,' said the oldest of the men, scraping out his porridge bowl. 'But I'm sure he's glad of the bed all the same.'

Jakob looked at Elisa's back which was turned on the room and her restless hands moving over the drawers of spices and herbs. He wished she would go. He had no proper idea, either, of what to do with these men who sat with heads hanging, shovelling down lumpy porridge while the boy lay curled up between them, teeth chattering, oblivious to the pillow Maret put under his head. Tobias was squatting down to collect up the broken glass in a pail. When he had finished he stuck his head out from under the counter, tugged at Jakob's arm and said: 'Shall I go up to the attic? I don't mind going if you want me to.'

'Put some more wood on the fire first,' said Elisa. 'You know we've got to get the place warm.'

'I've already been down and done it,' said Tobias uncertainly and looked at her.

'Yes, you go,' said Jakob.

Suddenly, the boy on the floor began to cough. The other men drew back as he sat bolt upright, his skinny back arching; they all looked away because his solitude was so overwhelming as he leant forward, gasping for breath with his hands dug down into the straw and bloody foam at the corners of his mouth, a fifteen- or sixteen-year-old boy far from home and far from all those who could have given him comfort. 'Look here,' whispered Maret, squatting beside him and holding up a corner of her apron to Jakob, 'when it's this colour it's coming straight from the heart.' The boy pressed his hand to his mouth and dropped back on to the pillow as limp as a withered flower, and she bent over him and murmured: 'Don't think about the tickle in your throat, it'll just make it worse.' 'All right,' said the boy hoarsely, 'I'll try.' Behind them they heard a loud crash as Elisa flung open the countertop and ran out.

Jakob had not moved since first entering the room and seeing the strange men, who were now lying down one by one without a word, wrapping themselves in the blankets and trying to get their heads comfortable in the rustling straw. The boy took hissing gasps of breath and stared at the ceiling with frightened eyes that glinted in the lamplight as Maret sat alongside, patting him. I'll go down and close the damper, Jakob thought. He reached out his hand and felt the warm chimney breast, but did not move from the spot.

'Aren't you going to do anything?' Maret asked, cautiously getting up and coming over with the bloodstained apron screwed up in a ball in her hand. 'Rub something on his chest to make him better?'

'Got no ointments to do that,' Jakob said.

'Something else then,' she challenged him.

He shrugged, but she stood her ground and waited, as if quite convinced that there must be something to give the boy, who lay awake among the sleeping men, fighting for his share of the air. 'You sit with him,' said Jakob and cleared his throat, 'keep him warm and quiet and I'll get him something later.'

'Will you be back, then?'

'Yes, yes,' he said irritably, backing towards the door. He felt the cold draught at the nape of his neck and stumbled over the threshold, through the office and out on to the steps where the winter air hit him in a blast of health and freshness.

He was tired of rooms full of sick people and had to leave her alone with her sympathy because he lacked the capacity to share it; he did not want anything to do with this new world of dead horses and wailing little boys, for he could not cure a single one and they would have to stop demanding it of him. He put his hand inside his collar and pulled it open so the air rushed in on to his bare skin; he tipped his head back and opened his mouth to the snow; he bellowed, making the sparrows that had crept into the thickets by the barn for the night go chattering up in a long line of confusion. He saw them, little bundles of warmth and feathers, descending through the darkness and disappearing, he saw the bar that had been placed across the door of the shed where there were no longer any carriages to be housed, he saw Elisa bent over a snowdrift, retching, her hands pressed to her stomach. 'Are you sick, too?' he called, pulling the neck of his shirt open wider with a sound of ripping fabric. 'Did you think you might as well be, while everyone else

169

was at it? Or is it the blood you don't like? I shouldn't have thought someone who likes brandishing knives about would go pale at the sight of a drop of blood.'

'It's not the blood,' she said, straightening up and wiping her face with a handful of snow. 'I don't run out to the yard and scream every time someone cuts their thumb.'

'What is it, then?' he asked, moving into her path as she went towards the steps, for he was unwilling as yet to relinquish his rage, so vast and vivid that it almost made him feel glad.

'Nothing you need worry about,' she said, and spat. 'Nothing that's any of your business, in any case.'

'Be careful,' he said, raising his hand, 'I can't take any more just at the moment. The reason I ran off that time was that I didn't want to beat you to death. I might do it now instead.'

'No, you can't,' she said, looking at his clenched fist as it wavered above her head. 'You could never hit me or anybody else, I know that. That's probably the best one can say of you. And actually it's quite something.'

'Let me be angry,' he asked. 'I'd like so much to know if it helps.'

'It doesn't.'

'You've infuriated me long enough,' Jakob said, but the strong, splendid exhilaration was gone. He knew he could never bring himself to harm that body of hers, so hostile and so full of secrets.

'We've infuriated each other,' she said, 'long enough.'

'Wait a minute,' he said, as she gave a shiver and headed for the kitchen door, her hands tucked inside the arms of her dress. 'If you go in, I shall have to as well. And I really want to stay out here a bit longer.'

'He's nothing but skin and bones, that boy,' she said, and nodded. 'But I've been up all night. First I ran round looking for the doctor and when at last I found him he said he had no time to come and then he made me sit up with an old man who had had half his leg sawn off and kept trying to pull the bandage loose. And then, when I got home . . .'

'Yes, I know,' said Jakob, 'you went up to Lars.'

'Yes, I did. Then I ran out into the street and found a girl to help me and Maret carry him down and lay him in the shed, but when we came out again they were just standing there waiting in the courtyard, saying they'd been sent here. One of them had to be carried and another was sitting in the snow, I thought I'd go demented. I've seen hundreds of soldiers now, they all look the same in the end and then you stop caring so much about them. They just stand there saying nothing, neither begging nor threatening, all they do is wait, on and on. It feels as if the whole of life is in ruins.'

'Come on, what's the matter with you?' said Jakob. He drew her with him into the light of the kitchen window, but it was only her voice that had softened, not her face and her body, which still had the same old habit of bracing itself to resist as soon as he approached.

'Whatever it is, you've no part in it,' she said.

'So you said, but I don't know what that means. Unless it's the same old thing, which I never could fathom. I got used to it, as used to it as I was to standing in the shop all day, but I never knew what was making you so angry. What was it about me you disliked so much you had to keep scraping the surface to see if there was anything better underneath? That scraping, I got tired of it in the end. I bet you got tired of it too, didn't you? But now you can't hurt me

171

any longer, I couldn't care less what you think and why you want to strip me of my bark like a log of wood.'

'You *are* like a log,' she said with a little laugh.

'And you're like a stone, though nobody knows it but me.'

'You'll soon go floating off,' she said. 'But as for me . . . I don't float.'

'There there,' he murmured as she squirmed beside him and trampled the snow, 'there there,' as if she were an animal to be pacified.

'He's lying out there,' she said, pointing at the barred door. 'He's lying there in his old shirt with all the patches. And we didn't even have time to wash him.'

'We can do it tomorrow,' said Jakob, but she shook her head as if she could not imagine there ever being time to carry out a task so superfluous as washing and shrouding a dead man. 'He's so alone,' she whispered. 'And I didn't find the boys for him.'

'You should get to bed now,' said Jakob.

'And you, what are you going to do? Run off again, get yourself drunk, go to the Mayor's house and eat supper?'

'I shall go and see to that boy,' he said, moving towards the steps to the shop.

'You do that,' she called after him, 'but if he dies it won't be because of you, and if someone sleeps badly at nights there may be many causes, not simply the person they sleep next to. Try to understand that what happens close to you doesn't always have anything to do with you. We're stupid to think ourselves important, when actually people scarcely notice us and we can't change anything, not even ourselves. Even if that's what we wanted, which isn't clear by any means. I didn't say that,' she shouted, 'remember, I didn't say I needed to change!'

'Have I got to think about that?' he shouted back. 'Why should I think about it?'

He stopped and turned, but she had already gone in and slammed the door. He immediately forgot her voice scolding him and his own retorting yell, and went back into the apothecary's shop where the men were sleeping soundly while Maret sat to one side, watching over them. She turned her sleepy Moluccan face to him and put her finger to her lips so he would not wake the boy, and once he had measured out drops of opium into a glass and placed it on the counter he went down to the cellar, raked ashes over the glowing embers of the fire and closed the damper. His feet crunched on the sand Lars had strewn on the floor and not cleared up after the last lesson.

On his way back he passed the shed and checked that the bar was properly in place over the door, then he stood there for a moment looking about him, at the white rectangle and its pattern of footprints, at the fence and the buildings that enclosed it, shutting out the view of the meadow and the mountain beyond. A single tree grew within it, an old bird cherry with rot in the trunk, which would need felling soon so it did not blow down on to the roof of the barn. This was the extent of his view.

He was thinking of nothing, not even of the man lying in the carriage shed with his ink-stained hands folded on his breast. Every word he had said and heard those last few days evaporated and left him there alone, mute and insensitive to everything but the murmuring silence around him, the impenetrable dark above the house roofs, the outline of the naked branches of the old tree, the snow that seemed so beautiful and harmless as it fell on his upturned face. That was all he saw now, not the buildings shutting him in, the streak of light in the attic window, the path between the doors that was so well trodden it had worn a groove in the stone paving, not himself. He did not exist. If he shut his eyes, nobody could see him. When he opened his eyes, all he saw was the sky.

But then he did go in after all, without knowing why, and climbed the dark flights of stairs to the attic room where Tobias sat dozing by a man who was lying in a stupor and seemed quite content. He nodded to them and went back down without having done anything, but he had to go through these last motions that meant nothing, these empty, mechanical motions that were merely a prelude to sleep. For it was coming to meet him now and he was longing for it, a deep, uninterrupted sleep. As he went into the bedroom he saw Elisa sitting waiting on the bench by the window, but there was no time to say any more. The long day was drawing to a close. Without undressing, he threw himself down on the bed, where sleep cascaded over him like a black waterfall.

He was on horseback in a storm that was coming from all sides, freezing his hands into uselessness so he dropped the reins, and lashing his eyes so he could not see. He had lost the flag. He felt the laborious motion of the horse between his knees and the jerk as it fell over and threw him into a snowdrift so warm he felt like staying there for good. There was a roaring from the mountain and the birds fell from the trees which were too sparse to shelter the men, who had broken ranks and were wandering about in the fog of snow. He leant against the dead horse and rested for a moment before straining forward and following the men across the lake.

There was no other way to go, but the ice could not take the weight of them all and the water was forced up over their feet, turning them into great clods of ice. Whenever anyone fell, they tore off his clothes and donned them themselves, so their route was lined with naked men; whenever a horse went down they threw themselves at it and hacked at the meat to get to it before the wind could render it rock hard and inedible. Everywhere there were sunken cannons that the horses had no strength to pull and wounded men, abandoned in their sleighs. The drivers of the baggage train sat stiffly, reins in hand, their faces contorted behind the ice. He had never seen people dying so fast or horses being knocked over by the wind and expiring as they fell.

When evening came, they made fires of damp, green birch twigs and threw on anything they had left, rifle butts and harnesses, broken sledges, sword belts, flagstaffs, flags and banknotes. They crouched round the little fires that were so reluctant to burn and fell asleep under upturned sleighs, died with their tinderboxes in their hands, as they talked around the fire, standing under a tree or leaning against each other. The snow buried them. The moon came gliding out from the clouds, as shiny as glass and as white as bone, and through the flying snow they saw six men who had frozen to death standing upright in a ring with their backs to the wind, facing inwards in an icy embrace.

At first light they went on along the route littered with empty sleighs and heads protruding from snowdrifts. The whole vast, open landscape was studded with the dead, waiting for morning which came with green skies and gusts of north-easterly wind and mountains emerging from the dark, more gigantic than they could ever have imagined. They ate raw meat and tried to peel off the gloves that had frozen to the dead men's hands.

Herds of horses picked their way through the long valley

and they followed, along a track that was soon snowed over and led them nowhere. He knew he was going to die, but he did not die like the others, those who could not resist the softness of the snow and the warmth that suffused you as soon as you lay down. He followed the horses, the cold light and the trees that had been bent by the wind and crept low to the ground.

He had discarded everything he had, everything that could weigh him down; he was wearing a borrowed coat, boots loaned from an officer who had still been mounted on his horse, a broad-brimmed hat that had come blowing straight at him, with a borrowed shirt torn into strips and wound around hands he could no longer feel. He walked. He would keep on walking, not stop like the others, not rest until the path began to lead downhill. As the wind abated momentarily, he could see that the mountains were beautiful in the sunlight which could reach only their peaks, not the valley where he trudged on through the metre-high snow. He knew he was going to die, but he very much wanted to live a little longer, a little longer, until the sun had risen a little higher, until the path began to lead downhill or until he could be sure there was no other option but to die like the others, be buried in the snow, picked clean by the foxes, blown away when spring came, scattered like a handful of sand to vanish among the heather. He saw his own shadow crossing the vast expanses and then the two boys, standing next to each other and looking up at the highest mountain peak that was floating in light above a wreath of mist. A grey bird hovered above them. He called their names, but they were looking at the bird and did not turn round.

He was drenched in sweat when he sat up and jumped out of bed. The room was empty and he ran out, not yet fully awake, into the dining room and over to the window where he could see Elisa walking round the big courtyard. She was marching. In her thin dress, with a cap of snow on her shoulders and head, she was walking round a trampled track she had made with her many circuits, and he rushed down the stairs and lifted her and felt her body burning ice cold against his own as he carried her to a chair in front of the fire. He blew on the embers and fed them with sticks, pulled off her stockings and peeled off her wet clothes leaving only her underbodice. He was still out in the snow. He warmed her to warm himself, for he could not forget the wind, how it cut and how it hurt. The wind was blowing from the north, carrying with it voices, cries, split shoes, empty uniforms with waving arms, hats that went rolling over the expanse of snow like black wheels and never stopped. Sitting on the floor, he massaged her feet and blew on her hands while she looked on in surprise.

The fire roared in the chimney and tinted the two of them red. He fetched the quilt from the bed and put it round her shoulders, then tried to dry the escaping strands of lank, wet hair that were hanging round her shining face. The whining in his head slowly abated, but Elisa was still shivering inside her cocoon and moved closer to the fire as he lit a candle and kicked her wet clothes into a corner. In one sudden movement she pulled out her hairpins and shook down her hair.

'Are you warmer now?' he asked after a while, at which she nodded, got up and went over to the bed. He followed her with the quilt and spread it over her as she curled up close to the wall with her back to the room. Sitting by her on the edge of the bed, he untucked his torn, wet shirt from his trousers while he thought about the horse screaming like a woman when it was knocked over in the snow. He had forgotten the sheet of paper Tobias had given him, the letter he had wanted to read in private and had carefully preserved between his shirt and his skin; it fell on to his lap now, and when he unfolded it he saw that the ink had run like raindrops on a pane of glass and the words could no longer be deciphered. He smoothed out the paper on his knee and bent over it, moved the candlestick closer and ran his finger along the non-existent lines. It was silent, the voice was gone. 'It doesn't matter,' said Elisa behind him. 'I can tell you exactly what it said.'

Jakob took her hand and held it closer to the light. Under the nail of her index finger there was a blue rim that no amount of scrubbing had been able to remove. 'You helped him,' he said thoughtfully, turning over her hand which felt small and soft in his own. 'He sat here at nights writing and you helped him with the copying.'

'He was tired,' she said, 'he needed help. It was so simple to help him.'

She withdrew her hand abruptly from Jakob's and began to study the ink stains that would soon be worn away. 'You don't know how much that means,' she said in a low voice, 'knowing one can. All I had to do for him was dip my pen and write some words. When you went off we felt quite lonely, both of us, but even so it was easier like that. Because you're impossible to help! He was so tired, and always so cold; in the end I lay down beside him in the bed, I couldn't think of any better way of keeping him warm.'

'There is no better way.'

'And it was easy to be kind to him. He was a place I knew so well I could never take a wrong turning. I knew the names of all the plants and found the path and saw the trees. There was tall grass. No sharp stones to cut yourself on and no bare mountains where the soil blows away, no wind. Not *that* sort of wind. I liked him so much.'

'Me too,' Jakob said.

He heard her sigh and turn over. He was sleepy too, and his arm had begun to ache again, as if it had a memory of its own. Dizzy with fatigue, he pulled his shirt over his head, tore off the dirty bandage, went over and threw it into the fire, but then caught sight of himself in the window and stopped short, like a picture in a wooden frame, half-naked and the colour of fire against the darkness beyond. He stood there scrutinising himself, his arms and hands, which he raised and turned in the little panes of uneven glass, his skin and the muscles beneath it. He observed himself as if he were someone else, but this was he and none other, this heavy, scarred body in the gleam of the firelight. This was Jakob Törn. The only thing that existed for certain was a body and the blood coursing through it.

Words vanished, words all vanished like little black dots in the snowstorm. He folded back the quilt, lay down on the bed and propped the pillows behind his head so he could see the fire, for he could not get enough of it. He was warm again, but the gale was still howling inside him. The boys had started climbing up the mountainside now; he could only see their backs and the bird flying above them. The big one had put his hand on the little one's shoulder.

'And that's the way it will be,' Elisa said.

'Oh,' said Jakob in confusion, giving a start as the image vanished. 'Has it been decided then?'

'Yes, it was decided up by the church this morning. The war's over and we're not going to have any more kings. From now on, everything is going to be run a much better way.'

'That's good,' said Jakob sleepily.

179

He yawned and stretched out in the bed, very cautiously to avoid her legs. He had no idea how long it would last, but for now and perhaps for a few hours more it was enough for him to be here, in the old room with the glow of the fire reflecting on the ceiling, with candles for protection against the dark and warmth against the cold, inside the thick walls separating them from everything out there so you could imagine there was nothing else but this: warmth, light, silence. He drifted in and out of sleep, far too tired to keep his eyes open but still not prepared to fall fast asleep because then the night would be over, all too quickly.

He heard a clock striking, a gust of wind sweeping snow across the roof. Later, much later, he felt the slight rocking as Elisa got out of bed, and he turned on his side and pretended to be asleep while he observed her surreptitiously, watched her standing in front of the fire warming her hands on the chimney breast, then crossing the room to the desk and opening a book. A chair scraped as she drew it up and he thought she was going to sit and read, but the next time he opened his eyes she had suddenly been transported to the window, where she was bending to look out and winding a strand of her hair round her finger. Her face had a soft, fragile look within its frame of hanging brown hair, her body had slackened now she was no longer paying such heed to it. Her hand moved in a slow spiral, an absent-minded movement with no end. He heard her sigh in the darkness and closed his eyes again, for she was just a person he did not know, thinking about something and believing herself alone. Yes, he told himself, she's standing at the window thinking.

He had experienced many things and many emotions, but never anything to match her restlessness. For it was still there

180

in the room, it would not sleep and it could not keep still, it fiddled with everything and talked to itself in a thin little voice. He imagined he could see it, as he had seen her attempt to bribe and beseech death by marching in the snow. It looked like a thorny stalk.

He had never understood either of them, he knew that very well, but he had kept them close. That was what he was good at, his only skill, keeping close without understanding.

They had understood each other, he knew that too, had spoken inside each other, gone in and out of each other like familiar rooms with doors always open wide. They were two branches of the same tree, but there was a point beyond which he could not go on imagining such a remarkable union as theirs, such a remarkable embrace of mirror image and mirror image. Then he had to leave them alone with the dark and the thin candle burning on the window sill, then he could only see himself, lying down close beside Lars because it was the only way to keep him warm.

It's the same thing, he thought sleepily as the images blurred in his mind, images of Lars, Elisa and himself. He did not understand how it could be the same thing and yet he was quite sure of it. The images ran into a single picture, he thought he was asleep but he was awake and could hear her breathing, over by the window. The bird came flying with its grey wings stretched taut like sails in the morning light. 'Are the boys still alive?' she muttered, and Jakob thought in his dream how strange it was that he, the one who knew nothing, could answer her question.

She lay down beside him and pulled the quilt up very carefully, as if she could ever imagine something so soft might disturb him. 'Why did you stab me in the arm?' he asked, and was nonplussed to hear the words he had never meant to say, never in his life, because he did not want to know why she had stabbed him in the arm.

'It was because you were crying,' she said, rolling and unrolling the edge of the sheet between her fingers. 'You came in and said the King was dead and the tears were running down your cheeks. You were so unlike yourself just then, and so like the you of long ago, that I had to make you stop. Because you didn't cry when your father died, or when your leg got messed up, you didn't cry over the children or when the boys went missing. The only time I've ever seen you cry was for someone you never knew.'

He propped himself up on one elbow and leant over the dark face on the pillow beside him. 'Are they alive?' she whispered. Her eyes were wide open, yet he was the only one who could see the boys in the snow. The gale tore through him one last time, he clasped her hands in his to make them still at last and said: 'No, I don't think so.'

Around them the town was sleeping, deeply and silently, as new banks of cloud built up to the north and came in over the low roofs. Hour after hour the snow fell, covering the dirty streets and the burnt-out fires, concealing the grey houses beneath sparkling baldachins and obliterating every remaining trace until the town itself was as good as gone, transformed into a soft raised contour between some rocky outcrops and a frozen river lined with masts and trees. Three thousand people or more were asleep in small, stuffy rooms with nailed-up windows and closed dampers, in barns and schoolrooms, curled up on hard floors or leaning against the sides of stalls. A third of them were soldiers with dysentery, fever from infected wounds, or plain, ordinary nightmares, tossing and moaning or sleeping stock-still because they had frozen fast in their memories.

Fourteen of them died that first night, and at daybreak the first coffins were loaded on to sleighs and driven off. The epidemics that followed claimed almost two hundred of the townspeople, not counting the soldiers who died in such droves that a new graveyard had to be opened. When spring finally came it was a sick, poor, ugly, hungry town that emerged as the hard snowdrifts melted.

The war went on for a few more years. The town was besieged on two occasions, once from the land and once from the sea, with fiery cannonballs bombarding the harbour fortifications. Twice, too, it was ravaged by fire, and destroyed so utterly that nothing within the outer walls was left standing. New kings took command. The old war was followed by new ones.

But no one knew anything of that just yet; for now the town lay in a deep sleep in the dark hours before dawn. The little room above the apothecary's shop was as rosy and warm as a summer's day, and Jakob Törn held his arms very carefully around the woman lying beside him in the bed.

He pretended he was doing it in his sleep and was not really conscious of where he was putting his arm or his hand, or of gently smoothing back a dark lock of hair and brushing a cheek with his fingertips. Under the cover of sleep he let his hand come to rest, as if by chance, against her hip. It all happened under the cover of sleep. He made his body heavy with fatigue, with his mouth in her hair he made himself blind and dumb with fatigue. 'I hope it's a girl,' he mumbled, pretending to be so sleepy he hardly knew what he was saying, 'I hope she has blue eyes.'